Jacob of Abbington Pickets

A Journey of Forgiveness

— a novel by —

H. C. HEWITT

Printed in the United States of America

Published by Author Academy Elite
PO Box 43, Powell, OH 43035
www.AuthorAcademyElite.com

Identifiers:
LCCN: 2020915996
ISBN: 978-1-64746-456-1 (paperback)
ISBN: 978-1-64746-457-8 (hardback)
ISBN: 978-1-64746-458-5 (ebook)

Available in paperback, hardback and e-book

Scripture taken from the New King James Version. Copyright © 1982 by Thomas Nelson, Inc. Used by permission. All rights reserved.

Book design by Jetlaunch, Cover design by Debbie O'Byrne.

Jacob of Abbington Pickets

Other Books in this Series
by H. C. Hewitt

There are family secrets that threaten to destroy Jacob. Along the way, there are many touching victories and, in the end, there is healing and reconciliation. If you enjoy historical novels with a touch of romance, you will enjoy this story."
—Linda Ford, fan-favorite,
top-selling author of more than
80 historical romances. www.lindaford.org

"In this book we are introduced to Jacob and the ups and downs he faces in rural Canada around the turn of the 20th century. Hewitt keeps the action coming and you will be holding your breath as you wait to see the next challenge that faces Jacob. Filled with rich characters and Christian values this book is a must read!"
—Karma Goodbrand - Her Good and His Glory

"This book was beyond amazing, sequel please? Even though the story does not take place in our time, it is highly relatable. It teaches us that hardships come and go and even though we feel we need to find out why, we must always keep our faith. This novel made me cry more than once, yet made me smile a thousand times more. You really begin to feel as if you are there with the characters. I will be telling all of my friends and family to read this book. No matter what you have gone through or are going through you will be able to relate to at least one aspect of this story and take something positive from it; I definitely did."
—Natasha Mercey, Surrey, B.C.

"This fast-paced read grips you right from the start and the story line never leaves you wanting! The struggles and emotions of the characters draw you into the richly researched and lovingly written history of the area, until it's the world that you enjoy slipping into every chance you get."
—Claire Johnson, Nanton, Alberta

"I was very intrigued by this book, which is the first in the series of Abbington Pickets. It kept me at the edge of my seat, as there was a deep, dark family secret revealed early on in the book. This made me all the more curious to see what would happen and how the story would transpire. I enjoyed each chapter and couldn't read it fast enough. I also liked learning about the main character, Jacob, and the various events that he experienced and how he dealt with them, including romance, mystery, deceit and tragedy.

Corinne Hewitt has become one of my favorite authors. She puts her heart and soul into her writing. She is not only a gifted writer, but also a very creative story teller. I look forward to reading more books by this author!"

—Amelia Griggs - author, Philadelphia, USA

"H. C. Hewitt's gift of storytelling shines as she tells the story of Jacob Hudson. In Jacob of Abbington Pickets, Hewitt transports the reader back to a small town in historical Canada. The characters are warmly written and truly come alive on the page. It is hard to not become attached to them. I shed tears for Jacob as he faced heart wrenching loss – and rejoiced when he discovered God's grace and love in the midst of heartbreak. My heart swelled as he found love, not once, but twice. I'll stop here and leave the story to the master. H. C. Hewitt's telling of it will both charm and encourage anyone who happens to pick up this book. It's time to brew a pot of tea, for, as Mrs. Rogers says, "tea is good anytime." Bert would agree. Once you finish reading this book, you will be eager to read the next two. What is in store for this young man? His life isn't easy, but with God, all things are possible"

—Tammy Arlene, author of Coming Home

"*Jacob of Abbington Pickets* is a book written from the heart. It chronicles Jacob's many losses from the death of his younger sister to the death of his father. There are many ups and downs.

Beginning the life of a writer,
loving your characters as if they were your own.
Your heart follows a fanciful love,
over hurdle, over obstacle.
Proving love, loss, and faith,
revealing a living soul with a flourishing character.
There's beauty in conceiving life,
and perceiving as it grows.
In another time, another dwelling,
places of emotion, loss of time, and joy.

-H. C. Hewitt

acknowledgments

"I can do all things through Christ
who strengthens me."
Philippians 4:13

I would like to give thanks to our Lord and Savior Jesus Christ for all He does for me and my family.

To my wonderful husband, Kenny, and our beautiful children, Chantal, Courtney, Jaymie, and Joshua: Thank you for all your love and support. I couldn't ask for better advisers than my daughters, Chantal and Courtney. Thank you for countless hours of reading, for every moment I asked you to "stop everything and read this..." and your inspiring words during this exciting journey. Jaymie, you always know just what to say; your words of encouragement mean the world to me. Thank you, Joshua, for letting me grace the cover of my masterpiece with your portrait.

To my mom and dad: Thank you for all your life lessons and teaching me everything I need to know to journey this world and showing me your never-ending faith in God.

To Grandma Carol: Thank you for answering for the countless questions I asked during this process. Even though many times you had to repeat yourself, I know you did it with a smile.

To Grandma Hartlin: You have been waiting ten years (or more) for this book; thank you for having faith in me.

To Abigail: Though you're not old enough to understand, I thank you for the use of your name to inspire the creation of your namesake in my story. When you grow up, I hope my novel will inspire you.

To my friends who encouraged me and listened to my rants about my creation: Lorraine, you have been a great supporter, always in my corner, and for that I am truly grateful. Cathy, thank you for your numerous hours of reading and editing; I am amazed by your patience. Your words of encouragement mean a lot. Leona, thank you for all you do for me and for your editing; you are always there for me. Thank you, Gwennie, for editing and beta reading for me, you are amazing.

Tony & Debbie Photography: Thank you for the best photo an author could ask for.

Thank you to Kary Oberbrunner and your team at AAE for all you have done to help me re-publish this book. Thank you to Debbie at Jetlaunch for your incredible designing skills. It was a pleasure working with you. Thank you, Marlene Banister, for helping me get the "right photo" to make the cover complete. Your work amazes me!

Last but not least, thank you, the reader, for giving my novel a chance to entertain you and possibly change your life in some way.

chapter one

1898

"Jacob!" yelled Mrs. Hudson. "Where are you, boy? I need you to go get some wood!" Jacob was just around the corner from the kitchen doorway.

"Yes, Mama, I will," Jacob told his mother as he walked into the kitchen. He was the youngest son, just eight years old. His wavy blonde hair resembled his father's. He was a good lad, always willing to help without being told, always wanting to please his parents.

Mrs. Megan Hudson was a short, plump woman with a plain but gentle face. As long as she could remember, she had wanted to be a wife and mother to many children. Her father and mother had brought her and her siblings from England when she was fifteen years old. Her father was an Anglican preacher, ministering in a small town in Ontario. Growing up, Megan had been extremely shy. It was a surprise to her parents when she met and wanted to marry Benjamin Hudson. Benjamin was a strong-willed young man whose family had emigrated from Germany. Rumour was that his father had a wicked temper and beat his boys when he had had too much to drink or when things didn't go his way. Benjamin had left his father and mother when he was very young and gotten a job with a storekeeper. He had met Megan at the store. After they had been married for three years and had two children and another on the way, they decided to move west to homestead and become farmers. They bought their first one hundred and sixty acres, and called their new farm "Crocus Flats."

Mrs. Hudson had no sooner seen Jacob than she turned around. "Go tell your Papa dinner is ready, girl," she said to Jacob's younger sister, Lucy. Mrs. Hudson bustled around the kitchen, trying to get the bread cut, the soup finished and the pie out of the oven. There stood Lucy, timid and shy, not one for words. Truth was, Jacob knew, she didn't want to go tell their Papa anything. In fact, she was afraid of him, as everyone was. Papa was a tall, well-built, frightening man. Even his wife was afraid of him. Jacob knew Lucy would dread the thought of running out to the field to tell their Papa it was time to eat. It was a good mile walk, and with her little legs it would take her much longer than the rest of her siblings. There were six children in all and Lucy was the youngest. Not only was she shy, she was what her father called "dimwitted." Papa didn't have any patience for having to explain himself twice. *Poor Lucy*, thought Jacob. His father thought of her as a dumb girl because she wasn't as intelligent as the other children.

"I can go get Papa," suggested Jacob to his busy mother.

"No, Jacob. I need you to bring that wood in for the cook-stove," snapped his mother. "Now get going!" She pointed to the door. "You too, Lucy!"

Slowly Lucy and Jacob backed away from their mother and out the kitchen door. Lucy started to make her way down the lane toward the field their father was in. Jacob made his way to the woodshed behind their handsome field-stone house. His father had hired local men to build the beautiful two-story house, complete with a bell tower. It was the envy of all the neighbours. Jacob looked back toward the front of the house. Lucy slowly disappeared into the distance.

Jacob picked up each piece of cut wood and placed it into his other arm. He tried his hardest to hurry; he wanted to catch up with Lucy. He knew she was afraid of Papa. As he ran back to the house, his left foot got caught on the step and he tripped into the front door, falling down to his knees. Pieces of timber flew everywhere. Jacob sprang to his feet, grabbing each piece of wood before his mother could say a word.

"What in blazes' name are you doing, boy?" Mrs. Hudson questioned.

"Nothing, Mama! I got the wood! Be back in a minute," Jacob said, huffing and puffing as he ran out the door.

"Wait a minute, boy! I need more than that!" yelled his mother.

"Yes Mama," replied Jacob. He ran to retrieve another armful of wood. He thought Lucy wouldn't be too far down the road by the time he finished. He could just imagine her taking her time and kicking the dirt as she walked toward the field. Jacob ran as he left the yard. She was further away than he thought. Finally, he could just see the top of Lucy's blonde head as he ran up the hill. Jacob could see his father in the distance, plowing behind his horse. He could see Lucy as she got closer to their father. Jacob tried to catch up, but he wasn't fast enough. Lucy started to run down the hill, waving her arms in the air.

"Papa! Papa!" she yelled, still running. Then, in an instant, she tripped and fell. Jacob called out to Lucy, but she didn't hear him. He watched as she stood up and saw pain on her face. He knew she wouldn't cry. Papa hated it when anyone cried. It was seen as a sign of weakness. He watched Lucy pick herself up, blood trickling from the torn flesh of her once perfect knees. She started to run again, waving her arms about as she called. Jacob had just reached a tall shady tree and leaned up against it, trying to catch his breath. He saw that Lucy had almost reached their father.

Mr. Hudson, a stern-faced man, was very strict with his children. His heart had been hardened by growing up in a loveless environment. Although Megan held the key to his heart, eventually his bitterness wore through. He never raised a hand to his wife, but that wasn't the truth for their children.

Mr. Hudson finally noticed his daughter. With an angry look on his face, he noticed her bleeding knees. Shaking his head, he kept going. He struggled to drape the reins over his shoulders and hold the handles of the plow with his gloved hands at the same time. He was having trouble controlling the green-broke mare. Lucy yelled louder, waving her arms side to side above her head as she ran toward him. "Papa!" Lucy shouted, "dinner is ready! Mama sent me to fetch you!" She continued yelling, trying to get his attention. The young horse, not yet sure of small children, started to spook away from the loud pitch of the little girl's voice.

"Stop yelling, Lucy!" shouted Mr. Hudson. This made the horse even more aggravated. She reared up on her back legs with her front legs high in the air, then came down with a sudden jolt and lunged forward. Mr. Hudson couldn't hold on. He tripped and fell forward, losing his grasp on the reins and plow. The horse was out of control, and ran toward Lucy. Lucy screamed, holding her arms over her face. The mare reared up once again, Lucy's scream frightening her even more. She turned around quickly, with the plow following behind. Within seconds, the plow knocked Lucy down and ran over her chest, crushing her body. The mare continued to run for a short distance, pulling the plow behind her.

Jacob stood in shock. He couldn't move. He watched as his father ran toward his baby sister, calling her name.

"Lucy! Lucy!" Mr. Hudson scooped her battered body into his arms and held her close. It was certain that poor little Lucy was dead. She was frail to begin with; she didn't have a chance. Mr. Hudson laid Lucy's lifeless body back on the worked-up soil. He wiped his forehead with his handkerchief, pacing back and forth in front of her.

What was Papa going to do? Jacob wondered in horror. *Tick, tock, tick, tock.* Time seemed to stand still. Jacob watched as Mr. Hudson once again picked up Lucy's lifeless body, carrying her as he made his way through the tall grass. *What is he doing? Where is he going?* Jacob anxiously wondered. He watched as his father walked northwest of the field. *Papa appears to be walking toward the old abandoned well*, Jacob thought, *but that's half a mile from the house; he can't be going there?* Jacob walked closely and quietly behind his father. His father's steps got faster and faster. Jacob could hear his breathing. It was loud and laboured. He could see sweat beaded on Papa's forehead and rolling down his face. Mr. Hudson struggled to walk through the tall grass as it entangled his legs. He gasped breathlessly once he reached the well.

No! Jacob screamed silently inside, *Papa don't!* He looked helplessly on, not wanting to be seen. Tears welled up in his eyes and rolled down his cheeks. Jacob watched in horror as his father took one last look at his sweet sister's bloody face, then lowered his arms slowly and released her. Lucy fell soundlessly down the dark, deep well.

Snapping back to reality, not believing what had just happened, Jacob sat down so his father wouldn't see him in the tall grass. He sobbed without making a sound. Mr. Hudson proceeded to run back to the field to retrieve his horse and plow. He found the mare just a few feet from where the accident had taken place. He grabbed the reins roughly, took the handles of the plow, and proceeded plowing once again. He plowed over the area where the tragedy had happened.

Jacob stayed where he was as he mourned the loss of his baby sister and developed a newfound hatred for his father. *How could he have done this?* Jacob asked himself. *Why couldn't he just say it was an accident?* He wasn't old enough to understand an event of this magnitude. *Poor Lucy, poor Lucy,* he said over and over in his head. He couldn't get her image out of his mind. Jacob finally crawled away from the matted grass he sat on and scurried up the hill. He needed to pretend that he hadn't witnessed anything. How could Jacob look at his father the same way again? *My poor baby sister, poor Mama,* was all he could think. It was so overwhelming that he couldn't stand it anymore. Jacob held his head with both hands. He wanted to scream, but he couldn't. He didn't want his father to know that he had seen what just happened. He could never tell his mother; it would break her heart. She would never get over it, being so sensitive. Jacob tried to rationalize the situation. Finally, without understanding any of it, he vowed to the Lord and himself that he would take his father's secret to the grave, not because Papa deserved it, but to protect his mother.

What seemed to be hours was just minutes. Jacob wiped his face with his hands to hide his tears and pretended he was just walking to the field for the first time. Mr. Hudson saw Jacob coming down the hill.

"Papa, where's Lucy?" Jacob's voice shook as he spoke.

"What? Lucy? I don't know, I have been plowing here, boy," Mr. Hudson replied.

"Mama sent her out over an hour ago to fetch you for dinner," Jacob said. "Are you sure you haven't seen her?" he asked.

"I said she wasn't here!" Mr. Hudson snapped. He stopped abruptly and unhooked the horse from the plow. He took the reins and walked toward the house. Jacob slowly followed, not knowing what to say. He too feared his father. He knew full well that his father was lying, but why would he lie? Why would he want to hide Lucy's body? Why wouldn't he just tell everyone it was an accident? After all, it was the horse that killed her, not Papa. Jacob didn't understand what his father was thinking.

"We have to look for her," Jacob said, with a quiver in his voice. He quickly squeezed his eyes shut, scared of what his father was going to say or do.

"She will be here somewhere, boy. She probably got side-tracked and went flower picking. You know how simple she is," said his father, with no feeling in his voice. He seemed unaware of Jacob's knowledge of the event that had taken place only feet away from where they stood.

Mr. Hudson and Jacob reached the yard, put the horse in the barn, and headed into the house. While they washed their hands in the basin on the porch, Mrs. Hudson took fresh buns from the oven in the kitchen. "Where is Lucy?" she called out to them.

"I don't know. Probably out picking flowers," Mr. Hudson said in an annoyed voice. Moments after he spoke those words, a big bang echoed from the kitchen. Mrs. Hudson had dropped the pan filled with buns on the floor.

"What!" Mrs. Hudson shouted. She went running to her husband, who seemed to have no concern about what she was feeling. As a blanket of fear came over her, her body started to shake. She ran outside, yelling, "Lucy! Lucy! Can you hear me? Lucy, Lucy! Please come back to the house!"

Mr. Hudson went to her and yelled, "Get back in the house, woman. She will come back. You know what a dreamer she is. She probably got side-tracked." He clenched her arms and shook her. "Stop it! Stop being foolish!" he screamed in her face. Jacob could see the guilt written all over Papa's face.

"Stop it, Papa!" Jacob grabbed his father's arm with his small hands as he started to sob. His father shook him loose, threw his hands in the air, and went back out to the barn. Jacob knew what his father was thinking, because he was thinking it too. They both knew full well that Lucy was never coming back. Jacob knew he was trying to put off the search that would be taking place very soon.

All the other children came outside and started calling for their youngest sister. It was apparent that they were distraught by the news of Lucy's sudden disappearance. Jane, a strong-willed young lady of twelve, a no-nonsense kind of girl, panicked as she ran around the house calling Lucy's name. Sarah, at ten years old, was selfish and thought mostly of herself and avoiding chores, but she too was worried that something terrible had happened to Lucy. Jacob's older brothers, Peter and Andrew, ran to their closest neighbours to ask for help. Peter was a shy, smart, sensitive fifteen-year-old. Andrew, an awkward thirteen-year-old, did everything he could to please his father. By sundown, the majority of the nearby neighbours were on foot or horseback searching for their precious Lucy. Mr. Hudson played his part. Jacob saw him yell out for Lucy just like everyone else. His mother was beside herself with grief. She couldn't understand what could have happened to Lucy.

"Could she have wandered away and fallen in the creek?" suggested Jacob's mother. "She could have gotten lost in the trees while picking flowers," she added. "Could Lucy have tripped and fallen and hurt herself? She is only five years old!"

Mrs. Hudson began to sob uncontrollably. Every possible scenario went through her mind. Mrs. Ford, her dearest friend and closest neighbour, tried countless times to console the distraught mother, to no avail.

"Please just come sit down and have some tea, Megan. Leave it to the men. They will find her," Mrs. Ford sympathetically suggested. It was close to midnight when Jacob came down the two-way staircase and saw the two women sitting at the kitchen table in front of the window. He could see lanterns glowing in the darkness, coming toward the house. Hope turned to dread when the men came staggering into the house. The looks on their solemn faces told everyone what they wanted to know. Mr. Hudson took off his hat and shook his head as he walked past Mrs. Hudson and left the room. She started to shriek and cry uncontrollably. Mrs. Ford held her and tried to console her.

Jacob came running to his mother and touched her arm with his hand. "It's okay, Mama. Please don't cry," he pleaded. Tears streamed down his cheeks. He couldn't help it. All he felt was sadness. His older sisters crouched down beside him and took him gently by the arm. "Come on, Jacob," Jane coaxed, "let's go to bed and leave Mama alone." They led him back up the stairs. Peter and Andrew, who had been out searching with the other men, washed up and got ready for bed.

Everyone stood in the kitchen, tired, cold, and hungry. No one knew what to think, say, or do. They stood there helplessly. Mr. Ford held his hat in his hand said sympathetically, "As soon as day breaks, ma'am, we will begin the search again. We will just get some rest and come back first thing." He glanced at his wife as he finished speaking.

"I can't leave her," Mrs. Ford whispered to her husband, holding Mrs. Hudson's head in her lap. He nodded, bent down to kiss his wife gently on the cheek, and left.

That night Jacob woke up and sat straight up in his bed. Sweat beaded his forehead and his heart pounded fearfully.

He had woken from a terrible nightmare. He had dreamed he was standing over Lucy's lifeless body. Then his father had appeared and began chasing him down the lane toward the main road. Jacob ran and ran without seeming to get further away, his heart pounding with a fear he had never felt before. He could hear his father calling after him. All at once he felt a hand on his shoulder with intense strength; he turned around swiftly and abruptly woke up.

chapter two

It had been days since Lucy's disappearance. Neighbours and friends slowly stopped searching. Every day fewer and fewer people came to look for the little girl. Mrs. Hudson's fear turned to grief and she shut herself off from the rest of the family. She sat in her chair in the sitting room looking out the window. She daydreamed that Lucy would come walking up the road, smiling, and carrying flowers she had just picked.

Jacob tried to encourage his mother. He was too young to go with the adults on the search but he tried his best to help his mother at home. He milked the cow and did his chores without being asked. However, he continued to have the same nightmare that he had the first night of Lucy's disappearance. It was always the same. Jacob saw Lucy, and then his father was chasing him, and Jacob ran and ran but never got further away.

Jane and Sarah took care of the household chores, cleaning, washing clothes, and making meals. Mrs. Hudson stopped doing everything, even speaking. Mrs. Ford stopped by every day to see if she was any better and to check on the children.

Mrs. Ford knew Mr. Hudson wasn't a kind man. She knew how he treated his wife and children. No one else knew. To those outside his household, he portrayed a good husband, wonderful father, and obliging neighbour. Nothing was further from the truth. He was hard on his boys, and expected them to do work way beyond their years. When it was time for a trip to the nearby village of Abbington Pickets for supplies, he would promise the children that they could go with him as long as their chores were done. He would always make sure they had so much to do that they couldn't possibly be ready in time. Then Mr. Hudson would go to the village alone, just as he had planned.

"Megan, Megan," Mrs. Ford spoke softly and held her hands. Mrs. Hudson continued to stare out the window as if no one was speaking to her, or even in the room, for that matter.

"Please, Megan, the children need you," Mrs. Ford begged. "Please make an effort to do something," Mrs. Ford continued. Finally, she gave up. She stood up and went into the kitchen to help the girls prepare that evening's supper.

"Is Mama going to be okay, Mrs. Ford?" asked Sarah as she stirred the stew in the pot on the stove.

"Yes, child, she will be okay," Mrs. Ford answered softly. "It's a hard thing to grieve a child, and the not knowing drives you to a place no one can understand," Mrs. Ford tried to explain. "Only the Lord knows what has happened, and to put your trust in Him is all you can do at this time."

"Thank you, Mrs. Ford, for helping us," said Jane as she started to set the table. "It's been so hard on Mama, and all of us. Do you think we will ever find Lucy?" Just as she asked, a knock came on the door. Jane ran to answer it. It was Mr. MacDonald, their neighbour to the north.

"Is your pa here?" he asked.

"No, sir, he has gone to Abbington Pickets to put a letter in the newspaper about Lucy's disappearance," Jane replied.

"Is there something we can help you with, Mr. MacDonald?" Mrs. Ford asked as she wiped her hands on a dish towel and walked up behind Jane.

"Well, Ma'am, I hear tell word in town that a tribe of Indians were through here around the time the little girl disappeared," Mr. MacDonald stated. "It's possible they took her, if they saw her walking down the road," he continued. "They say the tribe is headed for America." He tipped his hat and added, "Thought you should know." He backed out of the doorway, climbed on his horse, and rode off.

"Could Indians really have taken Lucy?" asked Jacob, holding onto Sarah's arm.

"I'm not sure, Jacob. We will have to wait and tell your Pa," answered Mrs. Ford. "Now come back into the kitchen and finish getting ready for supper," she said as they all walked toward the kitchen. Mrs. Ford didn't tell Mrs. Hudson what Mr. MacDonald had said. She didn't want to worry her or get her hopes up. All they could do was wait to see what Mr. Hudson had to say when he returned home from town.

The next day Mr. Hudson and four of his neighbours set out for the American border. After learning about the Indians travelling through the area, neighbours had encouraged him to search for them. Of course, Mr. Hudson knew that the trip would be a huge waste of time. He needed to get his plowing done, and his neighbours also needed to get their fields done. He couldn't tell them the truth, however; there was a chance that he would be accused of murder and hung. Besides, what would everyone think of him if they ever found out that he let his new horse kill his own daughter? They would conclude that he didn't know how to handle his own animals, or train them, for that matter.

"Be careful," Mrs. Hudson told her husband. "Bring our Lucy home!" She finished speaking, turned from the doorway, and went back into the house. She returned to her chair, gazed out the window, and started to cry her heart out. All the children tried to console her. As always, they gave up.

"Mama doesn't want to eat," complained Sarah, "or sleep, or talk, or do anything."

"Don't say such things about Mama," Jane said sternly to her sister. She grabbed her arm and pulled her out of the room their mother was in. "Be respectful!" Jane scolded. "Mama is having a hard time. She can't help it. We need to be patient with her. Now, go finish your chores." Sarah pouted as she darted out of the room to finish the dishes. Poor Jane had kept the family together since that fateful day Lucy disappeared.

Two weeks had come and gone by the time Mr. Hudson and his neighbours came riding home, with no Lucy. They had travelled many miles, to no avail. The eager and hopeful men found two Indian reservations, but there was no sign of Lucy. The chiefs of the tribes said they had never seen any white girl. That's what they said, at least. With doubt, but no alternative, the posse came home.

chapter three

Eight years had passed since Lucy went missing. The search reached a dead end. Months went by and everyone was forced to go back to their everyday lives. The land needed to be planted, the animals fed, the crops required harvesting. It was necessary to can food and prepare for yet another winter. That winter turned into spring, then summer, and before long years had gone by.

Mrs. Hudson didn't cope very well. She was never the same after the disappearance of her youngest child. Jane and Jacob were a huge help to her with everyday household chores. Sarah, in her unique way, tried to help, but always managed to get in the way. She was too wrapped up in herself, and found it very hard to focus on everyday life.

Sarah was now eighteen years old, and was turning into a beautiful young lady. The problem was that she knew it. Her long curly blonde hair and blue eyes guaranteed that she wasn't going to be an old maid. She wanted desperately to fall in love, get married, and move away. Jane, on the other hand, was so busy being practical that she didn't even think about getting married. At twenty, with straight brown hair and grey eyes, she was less attractive, and didn't have a problem with staying that way.

Peter and Andrew had grown up to be tall, strong young men, just like their father. Peter had dark hair and Andrew looked more like his younger brother, with blonde locks. They were now in their twenties and remained bachelors, though each now had a farm of his own. They lived a quarter of a mile from each other and their father, so it was still easy to help him, and they remained eager helpers despite their father's disposition. Mr. Hudson seemed to get angrier every day after Lucy's accident. Of course, no one knew about the accident. Mr. Hudson seemed to intend to take the secret to his grave.

Jacob grew up to be a handsome lad. His steel blue eyes and curly blonde hair made him quite attractive, especially when he smiled, revealing a dimple in each cheek. He was tall and extremely muscular, with a slender build. He had shown his father that he was more than capable of helping him with the farm at Crocus Flats, even at the age of sixteen. He tried his best to help his mother too. Sometimes he felt torn between the two. Jacob had great compassion for his mother and always tried to do what was necessary to help her. He knew how poorly his father treated her.

Mrs. Hudson had spent some time in the hospital because of her mental state after Lucy vanished. She was more distraught than when baby Allie had died at five months old, just before their beautiful stone house was completed. Jacob remembered what a sad day that was for everyone. It was Jane who found Allie lying in her basket, so still and cold. Doc Johnson said she just forgot to breathe that day.

Some folks say time heals a broken heart but Jacob wondered if that was really true. All he knew was his heart still hurt for both his younger sisters. He continued to have the same nightmare he had since that fateful night. He couldn't seem to get over his memories of his father and Lucy. Jacob was angry at his father and at God for letting such a horrible thing happen to his little sister, and for taking his baby sister.

Today was a special day. Today, the family was going to the church picnic in the village, Abbington Pickets. There hadn't been a celebration in the village since last July, when Saskatchewan had officially become a province. Today was the twenty-second anniversary of the All Saints Anglican Church and everyone from the village and surrounding areas would be there. In 1884, all the villagers had gotten together and built the beautiful church with a cement foundation, grey wooden siding, and a steeple, complete with a bell. The precise workmanship on the decor inside the church was done with true art. There were hand-carved pews with knee rests and a highly decorated pulpit in which the Reverend stood to deliver his messages. There were side pews adjacent to the pulpit in which the choir would sing along to the music from the beautiful pump organ Mrs. Smyth played.

It was always exciting to do something other than work. It was also a great opportunity to forget troubles and have some fun. Jacob's friend Charles Edwards would be there, and they would be playing horseshoes, or maybe even croquet. Jane, Sarah, and Jacob rode in the back of the wagon, while Mr. and Mrs. Hudson sat in the front.

"Hee-ya!" shouted Mr. Hudson as he whipped the horses to get going.

"Why do you have to sound so angry all the time?" asked Mrs. Hudson.

"Quiet, woman," was all he replied.

The children all thought that their father was hard on the horses, as well on their mother and them, but no one ever dared say a word. As the horses loped in rhythm, everyone in the wagon happily sang "God Be With You Till We Meet Again." It was a favourite hymn of Mrs. Hudson's. The drive was almost an hour long, and a rough one. They took along handmade quilts to sit on and all the food they could eat. The two-horse team pulled into the approach to Abbington Pickets and headed straight down Main Street toward the church.

Jacob saw his buddy Charles standing by his horse and buggy waving his arms to get his attention. Charles had been Jacob's friend as long as they could remember. He was a bit of a prankster, always with a joke up his sleeve. He was a freckle-faced, red-headed boy who didn't do very well in school, but he always managed to get everyone's attention by making them laugh.

Jane and Sarah spied their friends playing croquet. When the horses stopped, everyone jumped out of the back of the wagon with much excitement. Jacob kissed his mother before he ran over to meet his friend.

"Good-bye, Mama, see you later," the girls simultaneously spoke and ran to play croquet. There was a new girl there whom Sarah and Jane had not met before.

"Good day, Missy and Mary," said Jane with a smile.

"Good day, you two sisters," replied Mary. Mary was a smart girl who thought she knew everything there was to know about everything. Obviously, no one knew as much as she did. Missy, on the other hand, was a little bit of a tattletale and an exaggerator.

"This is Abigail," Mary said, gesturing at the new young lady who stood awkwardly among them. Abigail was the daughter of Mr. and Mrs. Rodgers, who had just moved into the big stone house east of Abbington Pickets. The family came from England and were looking to farm the land here.

From friends they had all heard the story about the three brothers who had built the huge house. The Benedict brothers came from a wealthy background. Their father sent them from England to Abbington Pickets to learn values and morals under the tutelage of Mr. Summerfield, who had created the village. All they seemed to do was spend their weekly allowance on fun and frills and sow their royal oats, so to speak. Once all the boys were married, together they had built a beautiful stone house and named the ranch "Goldenrod."

It wasn't long before their wives seemed to get homesick for their native country, however. As the number of horse races dwindled and the village seemed to get smaller and smaller, they packed their belongings and headed back to the United Kingdom. They left behind the elaborate twenty-six room stone house.

The house was built for leisure, not practicality. There was a billiard room, for only the men to enjoy, named the Robin's Roost. The ballroom hosted many dances and was enjoyed by all upper-class local men and women. Beautiful oak was hand carved in every room of the house, and there were marble accents in the furniture. If one thought the house was elegant, however, the horse barn was exceptional. Every stall was built with precision, designed with hand-carved oak. Every horse had a gold plate with a name engraved on it.

The Benedict house was abandoned because it was too massive for all the regular lower-class farmers in the area to heat. No one could afford its preservation, let alone chop enough wood to heat a house that size. The housework was a task no woman wanted to take on. When the Rodgers heard that it was there for anyone who was willing to look after it and pay the taxes, they took the chance. The house needed some work because it had sat vacant for quite some time. Just getting the rodents out so they could move in was a chore.

"You can call me Abbey," spoke up Abigail. "All my friends back home do."

"Hello there, Abbey," said Sarah and Jane simultaneously. "How do you like it here?" Jane asked as they noticed her foreign accent.

"Quite well, thank you," she replied, looking down as she pressed the wrinkles out of her dress with both hands, trying not to reveal to everyone how nervous she was. Abigail was not a shy girl, but she was not an outspoken one either. She had a pleasant disposition, but she wouldn't let anyone walk over her. She was excellent in school, which didn't leave much time for friends, as she spent a good deal of time studying. Her favourite pastime was gardening with her mama. Being the only child, she had many opportunities for adult conversation and events, and thus she seemed to be older than her years.

"How old are you?" asked Sarah.

"Sarah, don't be rude," Jane said, giving her a bit of a push.

"I was only asking," Sarah stated. "She looks the same age as us."

"I am sixteen," Abigail said plainly, with her head held up high.

"Jane! Sarah!" A voice came from far away. Jacob ran up and stopped, out of breath. "We are supposed to be going to the church yard to set up for the picnic." He continued speaking as he bent over to tie his boot, huffing and puffing. He noticed the new girl. Jacob was very drawn to her for some reason, and tried hard not to stare at her. He tried to look without her noticing. He admired her beautiful brown eyes, sharp jawline and the curly brown locks capturing her face. He had never seen anyone so angelic or beautiful, at least not around Abbington Pickets.

"Jacob, stop staring," laughed his sisters, throwing their heads back in the air.

Jacob ignored their comments. "Come on girls, let's go."

"Don't you want us to introduce you to the new girl?" They ran after Jacob as he walked away and teased him some more.

"We saw how you were looking at her." Sarah gave him a push. Jacob shrugged them off and kept walking, not wanting to show his embarrassment.

"She has a wonderful British accent," added Sarah.

Jacob continued to walk closer to the church, where Mama and Papa waited. The families all gathered around on the grass and their fine cooking set upon the quilts. The ladies all wore pretty dresses. What a colourful sight.

Rev. Young hushed everyone to say the blessing so every-one could enjoy their meal together. The minister was a great man, and was well respected in the area. He was the first and only minister since the church had been built.

"Amen," the crowd said simultaneously after Rev. Young finished the blessing. "Let's feast!" he announced.

When everyone finished eating, the girls helped their mother clean up the picnic. Mr. Hudson was already visiting with the other men. They walked around smoking pipes or cigars.

"Would you like to play cricket with us?" Mary asked Jacob and the girls. "We are going to play the girls against the boys."

Jacob's heart pounded. *Does this mean the new girl is going to be there?* he asked himself. *Wouldn't that be delightful if she was there. Maybe she would talk to him.*

"Sure will, Mary," replied Jacob. "Come on girls, come play," Jacob turned and said to his sisters.

"Aww, I don't know, Jacob. I don't feel like it," said Jane. "I am going to stay with Mama and the other ladies."

"Suit yourself," Jacob said as he and Sarah ran toward the cricket field.

Cricket was a huge deal in Abbington Pickets. When Mr. Marley came to the village from England, he taught the locals how to play the game. There was so much interest in the sport that the village set up teams, which entered into tournaments. Quite the sportsman, Mr. Marley also taught tennis and croquet. He had his own tennis court in his back yard. When he married one of the Mathewson girls, they even played tennis after the wedding ceremony, to everyone's amusement. They told everyone it was tradition.

Jacob's anticipation turned to delight when he saw Abigail standing with all the local young ladies waiting their turns. "Hello, Jacob!" The girls stretched out their arms and waved at him. Jacob nodded and tipped his hat as he ran past them. Shy as he was, he didn't dare look straight at Abigail. He stood with the rest of his teammates: the boys, of course. "Let's play!" said one of the young men enthusiastically, as he prepared to hit the ball. They proceeded to play.

Once the game was over, everyone went back to the church for homemade ice cream and lemonade. Jacob walked over to Abigail, who was sitting alone on her quilt under an evergreen tree. It was peaceful there, and she had seemed out of place with everyone else.

"Do you mind if I sit down?" Jacob asked.

"By all means...is it...Jacob?" Abigail asked.

"Yes, it is," Jacob said as he sat down with his legs stretched out in front of him. "And you are?" he asked.

"Abigail," she replied, "but everyone calls me Abbey."

He couldn't help but love the sound of her English accent. Her voice was like music to his ears.

"With such a beautiful name, why shorten it?" he said plainly. Abigail just shrugged. "I noticed you left the others. Thought you might like some company," Jacob continued.

"I am just fine, thank you," Abigail said abruptly. She had a cool disposition and didn't mind showing it. Jacob felt the iceberg she was giving off. *She seems to have a chip on her shoulder,* thought Jacob.

"I'm sorry to have bothered you," Jacob said shyly.

"You know, I am taken," Abigail said bluntly. "I am going back to England as soon as I am eighteen and I will be married." She looked quite refined as she arched her back while sitting up straight. *I might as well get that out in the open,* she thought. There was no point in making any friends while she was here. Her big, elegant, flower-covered hat made her look older than she really was.

Jacob was taken aback by her comment. "I only meant...I was only trying to..." Jacob stumbled over his words as he got up. He tipped his hat again. "Good day," Jacob finished and backed slowly away.

"I was just telling you," Abigail said loudly as he got further away. He turned quickly and walked back to the horse and wagon. Fortunately, Mama and Papa had started loading the wagon and were getting ready to go back home.

"Boy, where have you been?" Mr. Hudson glared at him as he ran up to them. "Well? I saw you with that girl. Don't even think about it, boy. Now get in the wagon." His father slapped him on the back of the head as he walked by to get into the wagon. Jacob felt embarrassed and hurt. His face was flushed and hot. He jumped in the wagon with the girls. Jane looked at him sympathetically and Sarah sat quietly. First Abigail knocked down his pride, and then, as an everyday occasion, his father had to complete the job.

Jacob felt as though the world was against him. His father never had anything good to say to him or about him. Jacob felt such resentment toward his Pa, even more so since Lucy's disappearance. He could never tell Pa that he was there that day and witnessed the unthinkable. Jacob never forgave him for what he did, but he couldn't say a word, as he was afraid it would break his poor mother's heart. The nightmares continued.

It was a long ride back to the homestead. The quiet was deafening. All that could be heard was the sound of the clip clop of the horses' hooves stamping the dirt road. As the horses pulled the wagon toward the house, Jacob, still feeling ashamed, mustered the strength to get out of the wagon and head to the barn to do his chores. His father followed two steps behind him. "Don't you be thinking of girls, boy. You will be nothing but a work hand and never leave this Crocus

Flats." He stretched forward and grabbed Jacob by the arm. "Do you hear me, boy?" he said as he forced his body toward him. "Look up at me, boy! Do you hear me?"

Jacob lifted his tear-stained face and nodded.

"What did you say?" The grip on Jacob's arm tightened.

"Yes, sir," Jacob managed to say.

"Don't you forget it," his father growled as he shoved Jacob away from him. Jacob stumbled and fell to the grass, staining the knees of his britches. He burned inside. He wanted to shout back at his father and tell him that he knew all about what he had done to Lucy. Jacob wanted his father to pay for what he had done.

chapter four

A month had passed since the church picnic. Jacob hadn't seen Abigail since that day, but she was all he could think about. The way her brown hair waved in the wind. The sparkle in her brown eyes. That beautiful English accent, which mesmerized him to the point that he felt paralyzed. Even though the feeling wasn't mutual, Jacob couldn't help but feel that she would one day be his wife.

It had been a beautiful sunny day. Jacob had finished all his chores and despite being fatigued, he made time for the one thing he had always loved: carpentry. He practiced his skills up in the loft of the barn. Jacob didn't want to be just any carpenter. He wanted to be one who created delicate furniture. His father didn't know about his desire and would have said it was a complete waste of time, but it was Jacob's passion to take a fresh-cut piece of wood and carve it into something beautiful. He had spent every evening for the past month on a tea table to surprise his mother for her birthday.

The silent evening suddenly got loud.

"Boy! Are you in here?" There was the sound of his father's voice and the clomping of his boots. Not wanting his pa to see what he was doing, Jacob hurried to the ladder that took him down to the floor. From the top of the ladder he said, "Yes, Pa, I am here." His voice shook as he spoke. His heart pounded. He started to swing his leg over to climb down the ladder and his father demanded to know what he was doing up there. Jacob reached the barn floor. His father pushed him aside and proceeded to climb up the ladder. "I wasn't doing anything, Pa. Listen to me," Jacob pleaded. "I am not doing anything wrong!" Jacob pulled at his father's arm, trying to keep him from climbing the ladder, but his father kept going. Jacob was sixteen and strong, but his father was still stronger.

He reached the top and saw what Jacob had been working on. "What is this?" he said as he lunged for the tea table and picked it up with his dirty hands. "Is this what you have been wasting your time with? You can't pay bills doing this!"

"Pa, please leave it alone!" Jacob pleaded. "It's a surprise for Mama. Please give it to me?"

"What did I tell you, boy? You will be nothing but a field hand and will never leave Crocus Flats! Now stop your daydreaming and wasting your energy on this nonsense." He took the tea table in both his hands, lifted it above his head, and hurled it past the ladder down to the ground floor of the barn. With a loud splintering of wood, it landed in a hundred pieces.

Jacob stood still, his mouth open, tears stinging his eyes. "Now pick up this mess and get to the house. Your ma is wondering where you are." With that his father climbed down the ladder and stomped out the barn door. Jacob couldn't move. He stood there in disbelief. *How could Pa be so unfeeling? Why was he so mean?* Trying to put on a brave face, he picked up every splinter of the tea table, loaded it into the wagon, and threw it in the woodpile for burning. His mother had a concerned look on her face when she saw him.

"What's the matter, Jacob?" she asked.

"Nothing, Ma. Really, it's nothing." He put his head down and his mother pulled him toward her and hugged him tight.

"Better get ready for bed," she said quietly. "You have a big day tomorrow. Don't forget to say your prayers."

Tomorrow the whole family was going out to chop wood to get a good supply started for winter. Even though winter wasn't near, it was a good time to start, because it was between planting and harvest. Winter might come sooner than they anticipated. Mama was the only one who didn't go. She would stay home and prepare the meals for the day.

Jacob washed up on the porch and headed to bed. That night he woke up with the same nightmare he had almost every night. He sat straight up in bed and sweat poured from his forehead. His heart pounded.

The next morning was another beautiful sunny day with a light breeze. Jane, Sarah, and Jacob got up earlier than usual, so they could get their chores done before they headed into the bush with Pa. Andrew and Peter came over to help with the chopping as well. They had grown into big strapping men with muscular, lean frames. They would be a big help with the chopping; the girls would do the loading. Pa hitched up the horses to the wagon and drove it to the front of the house.

"We are coming, Papa!" yelled the girls, as they ran toward the wagon. They knew how impatient their father was. Jacob wasn't far behind them. Peter hopped on the seat with his father and the rest of the crew jumped in the back.

"Hee-ya!" Pa snapped the whip and the two mares started to trot. The drive into the bush was a pretty one, especially this time of year. It was a grass trail, not worn down to dirt, as it was only used by the family. The trees moved in the breeze. Some of them had chokecherries hanging from them, but they weren't ready to be picked yet. That would be a job in a few weeks. The wildflowers were blooming, especially the tiger lilies and the lady slippers. Both Jane and Sarah would have loved to stop and pick some, but they knew Pa wouldn't stop. The horses knew the trail well and hardly needed any direction. The trail wasn't far from the main road to the village. In fact, the road was visible from where they cut wood. Pa stopped the horses and everyone jumped off the wagon, ready for work. The men chopped with their sharp axes and the women picked up and loaded the wood into the wagon. Several hours went by. The heat of the day brought sweat to everyone's brow. It was hard work for the girls.

The chopping of wood and footsteps were all they could hear, besides birds singing. Then the familiar sounds were broken by a strange noise. At first they could barely hear it, but gradually they realized it was someone yelling. A young woman's voice. "Help us! Help us, please!" the voice pleaded, as it got closer.

Jacob threw down his axe and ran toward the voice. "Jacob!" his father yelled after him. "Come back here!" Jacob kept running, not even hearing his father. He ran until he saw the loveliest sight he had seen in a long time. It was Abigail. She looked scared. Tears were streaming down her face and she was shaking all over.

"What's wrong?" Jacob asked.

"It's father," Abigail gasped, trying to catch her breath. "Something's wrong with him." She huffed and puffed. "He just fell over and then off the wagon. I can't pull him up. Please help me!" She grabbed hold of his hand and pulled him as she ran toward her wagon, which was stopped on the main road to the village. They both ran as fast as their legs could take them. Soon they could see the wagon. There lay Abigail's father. He was slumped over on his side.

"Grab his feet," Jacob told Abigail, as he lifted his upper body. They walked quickly, with baby steps, to the back of the wagon and hoisted him in until he was lying flat. Abigail immediately jumped in with him. Jacob sprang into the driver's seat. "Hee-ya!" he yelled to the horses. They started galloping at full speed.

"It's all right, Father. It's going to be all right." Abigail sat on her knees and spoke quietly to her father as she bent over him. Jacob drove the horses like a professional racer.

"Dear Lord Jesus, save Abigail's father," Jacob prayed over and over as they drove toward the village and to Doc Johnson's house. Jacob had not spoken to God since he was eight years old, but he had to do something. He felt helpless.

It seemed like forever before they arrived and Jacob stopped the horses in front of the doctor's house. An older man, not very tall, with white hair and a short beard and moustache, came running out. "What happened?" Doc asked as he and Jacob carried Abigail's father into the house. Abigail proceeded to tell him. Doc's wife, a distinguished-looking lady, was there as well.

"Put him on the bed over here," she directed. It was a one-room house, with just a curtain to divide off a small area for patients. It was a practical house, no fancy things. Mrs. Johnson told Jacob and Abigail to wait outside.

"But I want to be with my father," Abigail cried. Jacob pulled her back outside and held her to keep her from running back into the house.

"I will come and tell you when Doc is done." Mrs. Johnson gave Abigail a sympathetic look and continued, "It's going to be alright, dear. He's in great hands." She patted Abigail's arm and then returned inside to assist her husband.

Abigail covered her face with both hands and rested her head on Jacob's chest. Jacob, not familiar with a young woman's touch, felt awkward but good inside. He embraced her. Brushed her hair with his hands as he held her close. Abigail's hair was soft and had a sweetness he had never smelled before.

"Your father is going to be well again. Don't worry," he spoke softly. Abigail suddenly pulled away when she realized how close they were. As she straightened herself and remembered who she was, she said, "I am sorry, ah ah ah..." She didn't remember his name. "Ah..."

"Jacob," Jacob said. He stood there with his head down, feeling ashamed.

"Yes, Jacob," Abigail said, with her very English accent. Jacob so loved to hear it. Jacob realized that the intimate moment was very short-lived and far from the reality of their relationship. His father was right; he would be nothing except his father's field hand, forever.

For the next hour Jacob and Abigail sat in silence on the outside porch. Finally, Mrs. Johnson came outside. "You can come in now, Abigail." She spoke softly. Abigail jumped up from the porch step and ran inside. Jacob followed her. As she ran into the tiny room that held her father, Jacob waited in the main room of the house with Mrs. Johnson.

"Mr. Rodgers has had a heart attack. With proper care he will be well again," said Mrs. Johnson.

"Praise the Lord! I am so relieved to hear that," said Jacob, looking outside and seeing the sun go down. "I better go home now. It's almost supper," he continued.

"Wait a minute; Doc can give you a ride home," Mrs. Johnson said. "I know you brought Abigail here with Mr. Rodgers's wagon and you can't walk that far."

The ride home was long. At least for Jacob it was. Doc wasn't very chatty either. He was exhausted.

"Thank you, Doc Johnson, for the ride home, sir," said Jacob as he jumped off the wagon. When Jacob walked into the house, his father didn't receive him well.

"The hero is back," he said, without even looking up from his plate of supper. Mrs. Hudson smiled at him warmly.

"Your plate is in the oven, dear," she said. His brothers had already left for home. The girls sat quietly with their heads down at the table. It was quite apparent that words had been said at the supper table before Jacob got there. Jacob ate in silence. When he was finished, he kissed his mother, and went outside to do his chores.

Bedtime came early. Again, he awoke to the same nightmare. "Stop!" Jacob screamed. He had his hands on both ears as he sat up in bed, sweating and breathing heavily. "Dear Lord, stop these terrible nightmares," he said out loud, desperate to find a way to make the terrifying dream go away. Tossing and turning, Jacob's thoughts of Lucy and his father kept going through his mind. Then Abigail's face appeared to him, and he thought about how her father had almost died. "Thank you, Lord Jesus," Jacob said to God. He finally settled down and lay awake until daybreak.

chapter five

Another month went by quickly. Everyone was busy with the village fair, helping neighbours with odd jobs, and preparing for the harvest soon to come. Jacob was outside in front of the barn, brushing his horse, when he heard the sound of galloping. As he looked up, the beautiful Abigail appeared, as if from a dream. Her curly brown locks blew in the wind behind her as she rode toward Jacob. She wore men's britches, which made her even more adorable. Her horse stopped and Jacob walked up and put his hand out to help her dismount.

"Thank you, Jacob," she said as she stepped down. Again, her English accent made his heart flip-flop.

He blushed and all he could say was, "What can I do for you?" He stood there with dusty overalls and a dirt-stained face. *What a stupid thing to say*, he thought to himself. He tried to cover it up by asking, "How is your father doing?"

"Very well, thanks to you, Jacob. I mean...that's what I came here to do...I mean..." she stumbled on her words. It was apparent that she, too, was embarrassed. "I came here to thank you, Jacob, for saving my father's life." Abigail's voice cracked and she went quiet. Her eyes welled up with tears and she almost started to cry. She looked down at the ground, barely able to look at him, and tried hard not to shed tears.

She does have feelings, Jacob said to himself with a smile. "Aww, I didn't do anything anyone else wouldn't have done, Abigail." He reached into his pocket, found a hankie, and handed it to her.

"Thank you," she said quietly as she took it and dabbed her eyes. Once she regained her composure, she said, "Father would like to invite you to our house for supper tomorrow night so he can thank you in person." Her face lit up as she continued, "Please say you will." With that, she turned and put her foot into the stirrup and hoisted herself up on her horse. "See you tomorrow at six." She galloped away, leaving Jacob amazed by what had just happened.

Jacob heard the screen door slam shut and saw Jane come running from the house. "Who was that?" she asked curiously.

"Abigail Rodgers," Jacob replied, still a little perplexed.

"What did she want?" persisted Jane, as she stood there in her grey dress with her hair tied tightly in a bun. Jacob wondered if she would ever get married or if she would live at home forever.

"She invited me to come to her home for supper tomorrow night," Jacob answered, trying not to sound too excited by the invitation.

"Oh, my gosh, Jacob! Pa won't let you go and you know it," Jane bluntly spoke.

"He will have to let me," Jacob stated. "I'll have my chores done and then some, so he can't complain." At that very moment, Jacob made up his mind that he was going; no one, not even his father, was going to stop him.

The next day Jacob did all his chores swiftly. He even did extra. He spent the rest of the day helping his Father plow the new field they were preparing for next spring. He had to choose the right timing to tell his father that he was going to supper at the Rodgers'. He didn't know why his father always had to be so difficult and never wanted anyone to have any fun.

Jacob said, "I am going to leave the field early today, Pa." He continued, as his father looked at him with surprise. "I have been invited to go to the Rodgers' for supper tonight."

His father cleared his throat. "I'll be the judge of that."

"But Father, Mr. Rodgers is expecting me." Jacob's voice shook with fear as he spoke. "Abigail has told him I am coming."

His father grunted and said, "We have to get this field cleared."

"I know, Pa. We will. I will work extra hard again tomorrow." With that they dropped the subject until it was time for Jacob to finish and get ready to leave. To Jacob's surprise, his father didn't give him any grief about quitting work early and leaving.

He walked to the house, washed up, and changed his clothes. He said good-bye to his mother, went out to the barn, and saddled up his horse. He climbed on and headed out to the east-bound lane. Jacob took a back trail, which was quicker than the main road. In summer, this path could be used as long as it hadn't rained.

Jacob galloped into the Rodgers' yard from the southwest side of the house. The tales of this beautiful house were true. It was gigantic. The horse barn was bigger than the house, and the hired hand's house was as big as any regular house. Jacob was in awe of what he saw. It was obvious that Mrs. Rodgers had a green thumb; the flower bed exploded with colour. As he trotted closer to the house, the door burst open and out came Abigail in all her splendour. Jacob thought that the brown-haired beauty could make the rain disappear on a stormy day. He climbed off his horse and was welcomed by Mr. and Mrs. Rodgers.

"Well, my lad, you made it," Mr. Rodgers said as he extended his hand to Jacob. Jacob shook it firmly. Mr. Rodgers was a tall man with a moustache. He wore new britches and a nice new crisp white shirt with suspenders.

"This, my dear, this is Jacob," Mr. Rodgers introduced Jacob to his wife. Mrs. Rodgers was a slim, attractive lady; it was easy to see where Abigail had inherited her beauty from. Her hair was brown and wavy, and put up neatly in a perfect bun on the top of her head. Her eyes sparkled like Abigail's as well.

"Welcome to our home, Jacob," said Mrs. Rodgers. The house was as beautiful as everyone had said it was, far more exquisite than any other in the area. They had supper in the dining room just off the kitchen. There were fancy baroque curtains and beautiful lampshades. The table was set with beautiful china and silver cutlery. Bowls were filled with potatoes, carrots, and gravy. An oval platter held a carved, home-grown roasted chicken. Homemade pickles and fresh biscuits were a tasty treat. After everyone finished, Mrs. Rodgers served homemade apple pie with fresh cream.

"Jacob," Mr. Rodgers began. "We invited you to our home for a meal," he continued with emotion in his voice, "so we could personally thank you, with our greatest gratitude, for saving my life," he finished. His eyes welled up with tears. Mrs. Rodgers dabbed her eyes with a hankie from her apron pocket.

"You're welcome, sir," Jacob said soberly. "But really I didn't do anything that anyone else wouldn't have done, like I told Abigail." He smiled as he looked over at Abigail. She was teary-eyed as well.

"No, Jacob, if you hadn't been there that day, I wouldn't be here," Abigail's father insisted. "I want to tell you something, Jacob. I owe you my life, and I will be in debt to you forever," he said seriously. "I want you to know that."

"I don't think so, sir," Jacob smiled, embarrassed. "I don't think you owe me anything."

"If you ever, and I mean ever, need anything at all," Mr. Rodgers offered, "don't ever hesitate to ask. If you need a job, I will hire you. You can live in the hired man's house. As long as I am alive you will never be without a job," he finished. "Please, Jacob, if you need anything at all." His eyes pleaded with Jacob as if he would have turned the world upside down to please him.

"Thank you. I will keep that in mind." Abigail looked at Jacob with happiness in her heart. Without Jacob, her dear father wouldn't be here.

"How about you and I have a game of pool, my boy, while the ladies finish in the kitchen?" said Mr. Rodgers.

"Well, I really should be getting home," answered Jacob.

"Come on, just a game or two. It's so relaxing after a hard day's work."

"Alright, sir," said Jacob. Mr. Rodgers offered him a cigar as he lit his own. Jacob shook his head, "No thanks."

The billiard room was the men's quarters, and what a grand place it was. "They used to call this room the Robin's Roost when the Benedicts lived here," Mr. Rodgers said as he passed Jacob a cue stick. Jacob had never seen a pool table before in his life. He was a quick learner, though, and even beat Abigail's father on the last game.

Abigail walked into the room and said, "Papa, Mama says it's getting dark and Jacob should be heading home."

"Yes sir, I need to get going," Jacob said, as they put away their cues. Mr. and Mrs. Rodgers and Abigail walked Jacob to the door.

"Thank you for supper, Mrs. Rodgers; it was delicious," Jacob said as he put on his hat.

"Thank you for coming," Mr. Rodgers said, shaking his hand. "Please don't forget what I said. Besides, I could use the help. Doc's orders." Mr. Rodgers patted his left side, meaning his heart.

"I won't forget and thank you again," Jacob said. "It was nice to see you again Abigail, Mrs. Rodgers." He tipped his hat, lifted the latch on the door, and left. He climbed on his horse and headed westward. It was already dark, but Jacob didn't mind. He thought a lot about what Mr. Rodgers had said. It was late when Jacob got home. The house was in darkness. He put his horse in the corral by the barn and quietly walked into the house, trying not to wake anyone up.

"You're a little late, don't you think?" A growly voice came from the corner of the kitchen, almost sending Jacob into the air. He looked over in its direction and saw the light from his father's cigar.

"Yes, Pa. I lost track of time," Jacob answered.

"We have extra chores to do, so we have to be up two hours earlier," his father stated in a matter-of-fact voice.

"Alright," Jacob said, with dread in his mind. Of course his father did this on purpose. He knew that Jacob had worked extra hard today, and he intended to make Jacob pay for leaving the field early and coming home late. Jacob would pay for having fun. Jacob realized that tomorrow was going to be a long day.

Jacob got up early just like his father asked. He skipped breakfast and walked to the barn north of the house. He was expecting to find his father already there, but he wasn't. Jacob carried on and did his regular chores. An hour and a half had passed and still his father had not appeared. He had just finished milking the cow when his father came through the barn door. Jacob didn't say anything about him not being up as early as he said and neither did his father.

That was the longest day he had ever worked. It was the hardest, as well. Trying hard not to let his father know he was tired, Jacob continued to plow the field steadily. He knew that his father had done this on purpose to wear him out, knowing he had very little sleep. Jacob was not sure why his Pa did it. Maybe just to be miserable? Maybe to teach him a lesson? Whatever the reason, Jacob felt like he was ridden hard and put away wet. He thought all day about Abigail, and her beautiful brown curly hair. He recalled how she felt in his arms that day at the Doc's house. She had smelled so good too, like sweet perfume. He had never inhaled such an aroma.

"Are you listening to me, boy?" Jacob jolted out of his daydream and into reality.

"Yes Pa, I am listening," he replied.

"Well?" his father asked.

"Well what?" Jacob asked. His father smacked him on the back of head with the palm of his hand.

"I told you, you weren't listening," his father said with an angry look on his face. "You think you are so damn hoity-toity now that you have been to the Rodgers' big fancy house, don't you?" His father sneered. Jacob didn't answer his question. "Answer me, boy," his father yelled.

"What do you want from me?" Jacob yelled back. "You never want anyone to be happy. What is wrong with you?" he questioned his father.

"Nothing is wrong with me, boy," his father shouted as he shoved Jacob to the ground. Jacob jumped up and went to push his father back, but remembered it was his father. He was raised to be more respectful than that. He turned around and started to walk away. "You come back here. I am not finished with you yet," his father ranted.

"Well, I am finished," Jacob stated as he continued walking.

"What did you say?" his father demanded.

Jacob turned around. "I am not doing this anymore; you have no respect for me," Jacob continued. "I am almost seventeen years old and you treat me like a little boy." He turned around and proceeded to walk away again.

"You are so ungrateful!" his father shouted. "Come back here. I am still talking to you." By this time, he was yelling at the top of his lungs as Jacob walked back to the house. He went into the house and packed some of his clothes and other things he thought he might need.

"Jacob. What's the matter?" Sarah came around the corner to find him packing.

"I am leaving," Jacob replied. "I can't be here anymore."

"But what about Mama, Jacob?" Sarah asked. "You can't just leave her," she pleaded.

"What's going on?" Jane asked as she came into his room.

"Jacob's leaving," Sarah said bluntly.

"What?" Jane looked straight at Jacob. "Why? Where will you go?" she asked.

"Mr. Rodgers offered me a job," Jacob answered as he stuffed clothes into his bag, "and a place to stay while working for him. I can't be here anymore."

"Oh, my goodness, Jacob," whined Jane. "If you leave, what about Mama? It will just devastate her," said Jane.

"I have to leave," stated Jacob. "If I don't, Pa and I will kill each other." Jacob finished packing his bag. He took a few keepsake items. A little doll that had belonged to Lucy and a picture of his mama and the girls. He went into the living room where his mama was sitting in her chair crocheting. He knelt down on the floor by her. "Mama," Jacob said. His mother looked up from her handiwork and smiled.

"Jacob, what are you doing?" Her smile turned to a serious look once she saw his suitcase in his right hand.

"Mama, I have to go," Jacob started to say.

"What do you mean you have to go?" she asked with a concerned look on her face.

"Mama, I have to go. Pa and I don't get along, and it's getting harder to work together." Jacob held her hand as he spoke to her. "Please understand," Jacob continued. "I will visit when I can." He stood up, kissed her cheek and walked out of the room. His mama began to cry softly and the girls gathered around to console her. Jacob knew he was breaking his mother's heart, but he felt he had no other choice. His mother had chosen this life and it would never change for her, but he could make a choice. A choice for a better life. His father was at the door as he was leaving.

"If you leave here now you can never come back," his father said plainly. He did not show one bit of emotion. He wouldn't even look Jacob in the eye. He just looked down and kept walking into the house. Jacob left the house with an empty feeling in his heart. This was maybe the last time he would see this house, his family. His heart was breaking as well. Tears welled up in his eyes as he saddled his horse. He tied his belongings on the saddle and hoisted himself up. Jacob headed east down the dirt trail. The sun went down behind him.

chapter six

"Jacob, it's time for breakfast," Abigail called from outside the hired hand's house.

"Coming, Abigail," Jacob hollered from inside. Jacob had been at the Goldenrod Ranch for almost a year. He knew the daily routine. Early morning chores, breakfast, field work, dinner, fixing fence and other jobs, and then supper. Some nights Mr. Rodgers and Jacob would play a few games of pool before bed.

The Rodgers also hosted community dance parties on Saturday nights, when the workload was lighter. After all, the local masons who built the house had constructed a ballroom dance floor. The Benedicts had hosted many dances, as well as other events, for the locals to enjoy. For them it was all leisure, fun, and games.

Jacob enjoyed working for Mr. and Mrs. Rodgers. They appreciated all his hard work. He even designed and built a few pieces of small furniture for Mrs. Rodgers. But the most marvellous part about working for the Rodgers was Abigail.

"Good morning, Abigail," Jacob said with a smile as he strode swiftly though the doorway to the great outdoors.

"Good morning, Jacob," Abigail answered with a quirky little grin.

"What?" Jacob asked, noticing the amused look on her face. She looked like a cat after he's eaten the canary.

"What's that look on your face?" he questioned.

"Why, Mr. Hudson, I don't know what you're talking about." Abigail gave a pouty look like she was playing hard to get. She could still melt Jacob with her English accent, even after all these months. As she skipped along faster than Jacob walked, he jogged to catch up, then grasped her hand.

"Come on, Girlie. Spill the beans. What are you up to?" "Girlie" was a nickname Jacob called her. He had started one day when they were out riding their horses. He had tried to get her to jump over a small creek. She wouldn't do it and Jacob had said, "Quit being a girl, you girlie girl!" He had been calling her "Girlie" ever since.

"Papa says if we go into the village and get the supplies he needs," Abigail started, "and if we get back in time to fix the wagon wheel, we can go for a picnic." She looked at Jacob with a devilish smile and said, "What do you say, Mr. Hudson? Would you like to go on a picnic with this lovely lady?" Abigail giggled. "Beat you there!" She sprang forward and dashed toward the house. "Oh, no, you don't, Girlie!" Jacob chased after her.

"Alright, you two," said Mr. Rodgers as he came from the barn, just about getting run over. "Get in the house for breakfast," he smiled, trying to hide his grin. He was amused by the unique friendship Jacob and Abigail had developed over the past year.

After breakfast, Abigail and Jacob saddled their horses and hitched on their gear. "See you in awhile, Papa." Abigail waved. Jacob tipped his hat, nodded, and they galloped toward Abbington Pickets. The village was only a few miles west of the Goldenrod Ranch. It was a little quicker if you took the trail across, as the crow flies. "I'll race you!" Abigail shouted, as she leaned forward into racing position. "Hee-ya!" she told her horse. Jacob darted after her, thinking how beautiful she was right now, with her brown hair flowing like a river behind her.

Jacob and Abigail reached the village. They slowed and trotted down the main street. "Jacob, can you get the supplies Father needs while I run to the post office? I have a letter to mail," Abigail said.

"Alright." Jacob nodded and headed toward The General Store.

As he tethered his horse to the hitching post in front, he noticed his mother coming out from the building next door. "Mama!" Jacob ran toward his mother to give her a hug.

"Jacob, my boy," his mother cried out with a big smile on her face. "What are you doing here?" She looked up and down at him, as if to inspect his appearance. "Are they feeding you enough?" She glanced behind him as well.

"Yes, Mama," Jacob answered. "Don't worry about me."

"Jacob, I will always worry about you."

"How are you doing, Mama?"

"Jane and Sarah miss you," she said, avoiding the question. "Please come home, Jacob."

"Mama, I can't," Jacob answered. "Are you alright, Mama? You look pale."

"Yes, sweetheart." She hugged Jacob again. "I pray for you every night, Jacob."

"Thanks, Mama," Jacob said sadly. She looked at him with concern on her face.

"Megan, we are going now." Mr. Hudson came out of The General Store. He was gruff and pretended that Jacob wasn't standing there.

"Hello, Pa," Jacob said. His father ignored him and walked down the steps. He brushed roughly against Jacob's arm as he walked past him toward the wagon. Without helping his wife, Jacob's father climbed up into the wagon. He hardly waited for Mrs. Hudson to get in before he said "Giddy up." The horses started walking. Jacob's mother waved to him as they drove off. He knew she was crying. He could see her dabbing her eyes with her hanky.

Jacob felt so broken; he felt that his mother's sadness was all his fault. He still stood in front of The General Store. People walked past him with strange looks on their faces. Abigail walked up to him. "Jacob, what's wrong?" she asked.

Jacob snapped out of his thoughts. "Nothing," he said soberly. He had forgotten about all the fun they had been having on this beautiful sunny day.

"Are you alright?" Abigail tugged at Jacob's arm. Her face showed concern. "You're scaring me, Jacob."

"It was Mama and Pa," Jacob said. "They were here."

"Aww, Jacob," Abigail said softly. She knew his situation with his family. "I am so sorry."

Jacob was so grateful to have Abigail in his life. In fact, he didn't know what he would have done without her during this past year. She listened when he needed someone to talk to. She always had a smile on her face. She had helped him through tough moments after he left Crocus Flats.

Mr. Rodgers had also been a real saviour to Jacob. He allowed him to escape from his father's grip. He shared his experiences and stories about living in England and the journey to Canada. Life was easier in Canada; at least, that was what the advertising in the English newspapers said. Mr. Rodgers told Jacob, "Farming your own land is very rewarding." Jacob had become his own person, wanting to live his own life. He hoped to have a farm of his own, get married someday, and have his own family. He vowed to himself that he would not treat his children as his own father had treated him and his siblings. Jacob knew how he would treat his wife. He would not beat her down emotionally, but treat her with respect and loving tenderness. Jacob had learned in church, when he was growing up, that a wife is to walk beside you, not behind or ahead of you. She is to be an equal.

"Jacob, did you get the supplies for Papa?" asked Abigail.

"Ah," Jacob stammered, "No, I didn't get that far yet."

Abigail slipped her hand into his. "Come on. We can go get them together." She smiled warmly up at him. They walked into The General Store to get what they needed to fix the wagon wheel.

Jacob and Abigail rode back into the yard just in time for dinner. "Mama," Abigail spoke as she dried dishes after dinner. "Jacob and I are going for a picnic, once Papa and Jacob finish fixing the wagon."

"Do you think that's a good idea?" her mother asked, with a concerned look on her face.

"Jacob is just a friend, Mama," Abigail stated.

"Are you sure?"

"Mama, I know how I feel," Abigail said. "Besides, I am going to marry Patrick, as planned. I was going to tell Jacob about England this afternoon, when we go out for our picnic," Abigail continued, "but he met up with his Ma and Pa today when we were in town."

"Oh, no." Mrs. Rodgers gasped, placing her hand over her mouth. "What happened?" she asked.

"I wasn't there when they met, but Jacob was obviously upset when I returned from the post office."

"Poor Jacob," Abigail's mother said, "he's such a nice boy and to have such a father." She shook her head and continued washing dishes.

"So, I just can't say anything about leaving for England in the fall," Abigail said, "not just yet."

"Don't wait too long, Abigail," her mother told her.

"I'll do it soon, I promise."

"I just hope you know what you're doing, Abigail. I don't want anyone getting hurt."

"I know what I'm doing, Mama," Abigail reassured her. "Don't worry."

Her mother gave her a quick hug after she dried her hands with her apron. "Now, what should we pack for your picnic?"

Jacob came to the house looking for Abigail. "Ready to go, Girlie?"

"Well yes, I am," Abigail said. She stood in the kitchen with a big smile on her face and the basket in her hand.

Jacob took the basket in one hand and grasped Abigail's hand with the other. "Walking or horseback?" Jacob asked.

"Hmm...I didn't really think about it," laughed Abigail. "I think we should walk."

"Walking it is," Jacob said as they started toward the back of the barn and headed north. There were thick bushes in that direction and fallen trees to sit on. The grass was tall and crunched as they walked through it. Broken tree branches on the ground snapped as they stepped on them. It was a lovely walk and Jacob enjoyed any time spent with Abigail, no matter what they did.

Just then Abigail let out an ear-piercing scream. "What is it? What's wrong?" Jacob's heart was in his throat.

"Look! Look! Over there!" Abigail pointed, jumping up and down like a kangaroo.

"Where? What? I don't see..." As soon as Jacob said it, he saw what she was talking about. "Ah Abigail, it's just a garter snake." Jacob started to laugh and he bent down to pick it up.

"Don't pick it up!" screamed Abigail, clinging to his arm. She jumped up and down behind him, shaking in fear, as she pleaded with Jacob. He stood up and put his arms around her, gently holding her.

"It's alright," Jacob soothed. "It's only a snake. He's more scared of you than you are of him." He was still chuckling at the scared girl he held in his arms.

"I don't care! I can't stand them! They make my toes curl," Abigail complained.

"Your toes curl?" laughed Jacob.

"Yes!" Abigail shuddered at the thought of seeing the snake again. "Stop laughing at me," she said.

"Alright, alright." Jacob put on his serious face. "I won't laugh anymore." He was still smirking and trying hard not to break out giggling again. "Now let's get to our destination," he said as they got back on the path and kept walking.

"Over there." Abigail pointed toward a beautiful, enormous, willow tree with one branch growing outward. It was a perfect tree for climbing and sitting in. "Here, lay the quilt underneath it," Abigail directed.

"Alright, alright," Jacob laughed. "I got it. Do you think I haven't done a picnic before?"

"Alright. Don't get too big for your britches, mister." Abigail leaned over and tickled Jacob on both sides of his ribs.

"Hey! Hey!" Jacob twisted out of her grip and ran behind the next tree. "Oh, no, you don't."

She chased him around and around the tree, then stopped and bent over, huffing and puffing. "I give up, I give up."

"Alright," Jacob said, "let's eat." He flopped down on the quilt.

"Well, let's see here." Abigail began to empty the basket. "We have jam sandwiches, raisin cookies, butter tarts, lemonade, and apples," she said as she took the last item out of the basket.

"Looks great." Jacob began eating his sandwich. Soon every last crumb was devoured and Jacob lay down flat on his back on the quilt, holding his stomach. "I am so full, it's unbelievable."

Abigail smiled. "Well, my mama is a good cook." She knelt down and crawled beside Jacob. "Come on, let's climb the tree." She pointed upward.

"But I am sooooo full," he teased.

"Oh, don't be a baby." She pulled at Jacob's hands. "Let's go." Abigail stood up and started to pull herself up to the first limb. Her foot slipped.

"Be careful, Girlie." Jacob sprang up to help her.

"I can do it." Abigail climbed further up the tree. Jacob followed. She crawled up to the limb that grew outwards and edged across it, straddling the branch. With a leg on either side, she locked her legs together to hold her position. Jacob followed suit, facing Abigail.

"It's so beautiful up here," Abigail said, breathing in the fresh air. "I could stay here forever." Closing her eyes, she thought for a second about her life.

"God did create a beautiful world, that's for sure," Jacob added.

"What do you want to do with your life, Jacob?" Abigail asked with a serious look on her face. "I mean, do you want to get married? Do you want children? Are you going to be a farmer?"

"Yes, I want all of those things, Girlie," Jacob said. "But not just any wife. She's going to be very special, and she will really be loved." Jacob looked at Abigail with love in his heart.

Abigail started feeling guilty for not having told Jacob that she was leaving in the fall. "Jacob," she started. "I have to tell you something."

"What is it?" Jacob asked. "You look worried."

"Just something," she began, "I should have told you..."

Suddenly Abigail lost her balance. She swung her arms upwards to catch herself. Jacob quickly lunged forward to grab her, but her hands slipped past his and she fell backward. Her body flipped upside down and she landed on the grass below on her side, crushing her right shoulder and leg.

"Abigail! Abigail!" Jacob yelled. He climbed down the tree as fast as his legs would take him. He knelt down next to her on the ground. "Are you alright?" He touched her side and tried to turn her over.

"Ooouuuch!" Abigail cried. "I can't move, Jacob. It hurts so much."

"Just stay still," Jacob said. "Don't move. Promise me you won't move," he pleaded. "I will go get your father."

"NO, Jacob! Please don't leave me," Abigail pleaded.

"I have to. Please, Girlie." Jacob put the quilt they had been using for the picnic over her to keep her warm while he was gone. "I will be right back, as fast as I can." Jacob didn't want to leave her, but there was no other choice. He couldn't carry her and they didn't have a horse there. He ran as fast as he could through the tall grass that whipped at his legs. Branches broke as he stepped on them. It didn't take him long to get to the house.

"Mr. Rodgers! Mrs. Rodgers!" Jacob ran into the house yelling as loud as he could. Racing from room to room looking for them.

"Jacob, what's wrong?" Mrs. Rodgers asked as she came out of the library.

"It's Abigail," Jacob gasped. "She's hurt. We have to get the horse and wagon."

"Her father is in the barn," she said.

"Go get Doc from Abbington Pickets," Jacob ordered. "I will get Mr. Rodgers so we can get Abigail. We will meet you back here."

They both ran to the barn. Mrs. Rodgers saddled her horse, mounted, and started off toward the village. Mr. Rodgers helped Jacob hitch up the wagon.

"Over that way," Jacob pointed as Mr. Rodgers steered the wagon. It was a bumpy ride, because there wasn't an actual buggy trail. "There! Under that tree." Jacob pointed to the willow tree.

"Abigail!" Jacob jumped off the wagon before it was stopped and ran toward her. Her father followed.

"Sweetheart," her father said, "are you alright?" He knelt down beside her.

"Papa," Abigail groaned. "It hurts."

"Where does it hurt?" he asked.

"My shoulder, my leg."

"Jacob, let's wrap her tightly in the quilt," Mr. Rodgers suggested, "then we can carry her to the wagon without jostling her too much." Jacob and Mr. Rodgers carried her to the wagon as gently as they could. The ride home wasn't very comfortable for Abigail. She cried out in pain the entire trip. As they pulled up to the house, they saw Doc and Mrs. Rodgers waiting for them.

"Careful not to move her too much, until we know what's been damaged," Doc said. The four of them lifted Abigail out of the wagon and carried her into the house. They laid her down on the bed so Doc could examine her.

"Abigail," her mother said softly. "Mama's here."

"Thank you, Mama." Abigail winced. "I am so stupid, falling out of a tree."

"It's alright," her mother reassured her. "Doc will fix you up." She placed a wet cloth on Abigail's forehead.

Jacob and Mr. Rodgers waited in the family room while Mrs. Rodgers and Doc checked Abigail over.

After several hours and many cries from Abigail, Doc finally came out of the room.

"Well, she's badly dislocated her shoulder," Doc started, "and fractured her femur."

"What's a femur?" Jacob asked.

"It's her upper leg bone," Doc explained. "I wrapped it firmly and braced it, and put her shoulder back in place."

"What can we do for her?" asked her father.

"Just keep her still and make sure she gets plenty of rest," Doc explained.

"Can I go see her?" Jacob requested. "I need to see her."

"Yes," Doc said, "but not for too long. She is in a lot of pain. She may be a little grumpy but I gave her something for the pain."

Mr. Rodgers and Jacob went in to see Abigail. "How are you, Girlie?" Jacob tried to brighten her mood. He brought a handful of wildflowers and a big smile for her. Abigail smiled a sleepy smile and thanked him for his thoughtfulness.

Jacob hadn't been this scared since Lucy's accident. Memories of Lucy had come flooding back while Jacob was running to the house for help. He had worried that he wouldn't be able to help Abigail. He had felt as helpless today as he had on that day nine years ago. Jacob went to bed that night with his thoughts churning. *What if something had happened to Abigail? How would he live with himself?* He dozed off when daybreak neared, only to abruptly awaken, sitting straight up in bed. Sweat rolled down his face and neck. He hadn't had this nightmare as often since he moved away from home. Just every now and again, but today it was as vivid as the first time. *When would he be free from the terror of that day? When would he find peace?*

chapter seven

Spring was over. All the fields had been plowed and planted, the vegetable gardens put in, and the flower beds were blooming. It was summer, a great time of year. The poplar trees were in leaf, the grass was as green as emeralds. Butterflies floated about. The creeks flowed and frogs jumped through them. Jacob had worked hard all spring with Mr. Rodgers. Since Abigail's fall, he had done everything he could to make up for the accident. He felt it was his fault. When he wasn't working for Abigail's father, he did odd jobs for Abigail and Mrs. Rodgers. He managed to do everything from grooming her horse to working in the garden. Abigail's leg was healing nicely. She still had to stay off her feet, though, which meant that she wasn't much help to her ma.

Jacob had constructed a chair-type bed with wheels for Abigail, so he could wheel her outside for fresh air. She could also go out to see what everyone was doing, especially when Jacob and her mother gardened together. Abigail watched and had a little input on what went where in the flower beds.

"What do you think of these, Abigail?" her mother asked as she held fuchsia-coloured petunias she had just cut.

"Those are beautiful, Mama." Abigail beamed. "They will look great on the kitchen table."

"That's what I was thinking too." Her mother smiled.

"Mama," Abigail said.

"Yes, dear."

"I was thinking."

"Yes?"

"I am going to tell Jacob after supper tonight."

"So soon?" her mother asked, knowing that Abigail was talking about going to England. "You are just starting to heal. Maybe you should wait."

"I need to, Mama. I know every day he feels closer to me, and I have to be honest with him. The sooner the better."

"Well, if you are sure."

"Sure about what?" Jacob came from around the back of the house.

"Sure, ah..." Abigail stammered, "that we are going to make a cake for Pa for supper tonight."

"Oh," Jacob said. "Chocolate cake does sound mighty good." Jacob smiled and grabbed the handles of Abigail's chair and pushed her in a little circle, as if to twirl her around.

"Well then, Mr. Hudson," said Abigail, "you had better wheel me into the house so I can get started."

"As you wish, Miss Abigail," Jacob said in a pretend formal voice.

"Yes, we better wash up," added Mrs. Rodgers. "Don't you still have work to do, Jacob?" she asked.

"Yes, Mrs. Rodgers. Mr. Rodgers sent me to the house for some more drinking water," Jacob explained. "Ah...and maybe some cookies?" he added sheepishly.

Mrs. Rodgers laughed. "Of course you can take some cookies." She had started to love Jacob as if he were her own. He was such a fun-loving young man that she could never understand why his father wouldn't let him back in their lives.

Once they were in the house, Mrs. Rodgers sent Jacob on his way, back to work with snacks in one hand and water in the other. She and Abigail started making supper, including the chocolate cake.

Afternoon soon turned to evening, and after supper Jacob pushed Abigail's chair outside for a walk. They weren't able to go to their special place because the wheels on the chair couldn't roll through the tall grass and small twigs on the ground, so they stayed on the dirt road that travelled toward the village. Jacob walked slowly along, making the time spent with Abigail longer. They listened to the sound of the wheels rolling in the dirt as he pushed her.

"It's such a beautiful evening," Abigail said dreamily. "England doesn't have such wonderful sunsets like the prairies do."

"You are right, girlie girl." Jacob smiled as he breathed in the summer air. "It's as beautiful as the sight I see every day."

Abigail didn't know what to say. She could feel Jacob's eyes on her. This was what she had been trying to avoid. He couldn't fall in love with her.

"Jacob," Abigail said as her heart pounded.

"Yes, Girlie?" Jacob stopped pushing her and knelt down beside her. He looked at Abigail's hair, in a side braid down the left side of her chest. His heart yearned for her. He could hardly contain how he really felt.

"Jacob," she repeated. "I know when we first met, I wasn't very nice to you."

"I know," smiled Jacob, "but I knew I could melt the iceberg." He laughed.

"I am sorry for that, Jacob," Abigail said seriously.

"It's alright." Jacob recognized her sober tone. "Don't lose any sleep over it, Girlie." Jacob was a different person now. He had grown into a strong young man as time passed.

"I have something to tell you," Abigail started. "I don't know how to begin."

"It can't be that bad." Jacob was starting to get worried.

"We have become such good friends, Jacob," she continued. "I never thought it possible when I first met you."

"We sure know how to have a good time," Jacob added, remembering all the happy times they had spent together.

"Listen to me, Jacob." Abigail took a deep breath. "I am leaving," she blurted out.

"What?" Jacob gasped, jumped up, and stepped backward. "What do you mean, leaving?"

"Remember the day we first met and I told you I was taken?"

"You were serious about that?"

"I wasn't joking, Jacob," she said. "His name is Patrick." Jacob could hardly believe his ears. He was in shock.

"We grew up together, went to school together, did everything together," Abigail tried to explain. "When my parents announced they were going to Canada, I cried, begged, pleaded, did everything to make them change their minds."

Jacob listened in silence. He couldn't say anything. He didn't know what to say.

"Patrick and I were in love. We didn't want to be apart," she continued. "Nothing we said would change Papa's mind. I wasn't a very cheerful girl coming to Canada. Before we left, I vowed to Patrick that when I turned eighteen, I would come back to England and we would be married," Abigail finished.

"Wow!" That was all Jacob could say as he stood and looked down at Abigail. She looked up at him with sad brown eyes and a regretful look on her face.

"You have to do what you promised," Jacob said plainly.

Surprised by his remark, Abigail said, "I will miss you, Jacob. You have been my one and only friend here."

Jacob's heart was breaking in two, though he didn't want to show it. Obviously, Abigail didn't feel the way he did. He didn't want to ruin it for her. He wanted to be strong, even if he was crushed inside. "I will always be your friend, Abigail,"

Jacob said, reassuringly. "We can write, and soon you will forget all about me," he tried to joke.

"Jacob, I could never forget you," Abigail scolded. "And don't you forget it."

"When are you leaving?" he asked.

"As soon as my leg is healed enough," she said. "I wanted to tell you sooner, but then with my accident..." She turned her head away, not wanting to explain any more.

"Well, we will have to make the most of our time together." Jacob tried to be cheery. He pulled her chair backward and circled around to head back to the house. It was all he could do to pretend he wasn't hurting.

That night Jacob lay in his bed thinking about Abigail and her undeniable beauty. He thought about the way she curled her upper lip when she laughed. He remembered how soft her hair was the first time he embraced her when her father was ill. She had such sparkly brown eyes, and her accent melted his heart. Oh, how he would miss her when she left.

chapter eight

Harvest came quicker than Jacob wanted, since he knew that after the harvest Abigail would leave. Jacob drove the binder to cut the wheat and make it into sheaves. Mr. Rodgers hired four neighbouring boys to help stook the wheat. It took several weeks of hot sun before the stooks were ripe enough to thresh. When the stooks were ready to be threshed, Mr. Rodgers drove the horses pulling the hay rack while Jacob picked up the stooks and tossed them onto the rack. Abigail walked out to the field and brought them water to drink and cookies to eat between meals.

Once all the stooks had been gathered in the same spot, the neighbours came and threshed for many days. Abigail and her mother worked just as hard as the men. They cooked every meal for at least ten men. They would get the dishes washed, dried, and put away, then start over again for the next meal. The surrounding farmers took turns at each other's farms until everyone's harvest was finished.

"Mama," Abigail said, rubbing her hands, "I am so tired of washing dishes."

Mrs. Rodgers, who was taking a break in her rocking chair in the corner of the kitchen, wiped her hands on her apron. "Yes, if I never see another dish, it will be too soon." She smiled tiredly.

"Mama, are you happy here?" Abigail asked her.

"It's a different life," her mother answered. "That's for sure. Not everyone could do it, but your father loves it so much."

"Was it what you thought it would be like?"

"No." She put her head down and shook it. "However, I stand behind your father, and will never complain." Abigail felt a little ashamed of herself. She didn't want to leave her mother with all the work when she went back to England.

"Well, this isn't buying the baby shoes and winter's coming," her mother said matter-of-factly. She was always one for quoting English sayings.

Abigail laughed. "You do have a way of explaining things."

"Let's get supper on its way," Mrs. Rodgers said. "This is the last day of harvest for us, so we should make it special."

"Since it's a special day," Abigail said bashfully, "could we serve the fancy wine we brought with us from England?"

"I don't know..." her mother hesitated.

"Come on, Mama," Abigail pleaded. "Like you said, it is a special occasion." She smiled her prize-winning smile.

Mrs. Rodgers gave in.

"You're right." She walked to the cubbyhole hidden in the kitchen floor beneath the table. It was the perfect place to store the wine, as it was dark and cool.

"It's a great wine," she said as she held up the dark wine bottle. "King Edward himself drinks this wine. Did you know that?"

"Yes, Mama," Abigail laughed. "You tell me that every time we talk about it."

"We have three more bottles. I imagine we will need them all for the amount of people who are here."

During supper, everyone gathered around the big rectangular table. Mr. Rodgers stood up. "Mrs. Rodgers and I would like to thank everyone for helping to finish the harvest." He looked at Jacob. "Thank you, Jacob. Without you we would never have gotten this far." He lifted his wine glass in the air to toast. "Now, here's to a year of family, friends and a great 1907 harvest."

Everyone lifted and touched their glasses. *Ting, ting, ting*, they tinkled. Jacob and Abigail looked at each other and smiled with the satisfaction of a job well done. Abigail sipped her wine. She savoured the flavour.

Once dessert was finished, the neighbours left for home. It had been a very long day. Abigail and her mother finished the dishes and cleaned up the kitchen. They were exhausted.

"I'm going to go for a walk before bed, to breathe in the fresh air a little," Abigail told her mother, and she left the house.

Jacob stayed and visited with Mr. Rodgers for a while. They discussed the next year's crop and ways of improving planting in the spring. Jacob was starting to get tired.

"Mrs. Rodgers, thank you again for a wonderful supper," Jacob said. "See you in the morning. Good night."

"Good night, Jacob," Mr. and Mrs. Rodgers said simultaneously. Jacob headed to the hired hand's house. He reached the barn and saw Abigail.

"Abigail," he spoke.

Abigail just about jumped out of her skin as she whirled around. "Jacob!" she said, "You scared me to death."

"Sorry, Girlie," Jacob said. "I didn't mean to. Where have you been?"

"I was just out for a walk before bed," she said, trying to stand still. There was a little slur in her voice.

"Oh, really, and why wasn't I invited?" Jacob teased.

"Well, umm, well," she stammered, not wanting to explain what she had been doing.

"I am only teasing," he laughed. "I had a great visit with your pa tonight."

"Thaaat's gooood," she said as she wobbled side to side.

"Are you all right, Girlie?" he asked. "Why are you talking weird?"

"Jacob, Jacob, Jacob," she said, putting her arms around his neck. "You're my Jaky, Jaky, Jaky." She threw her head back and laughed.

Jacob could smell the wine on her breath and grabbed her hands from behind his neck. He placed them down beside her and she reached up and put them back around his neck and then fell into his chest. She almost knocked him over.

"Oh boy, Abigail," Jacob said. "I think you have had too much wine."

"I didn't have that much," Abigail slurred and giggled some more. She lifted her head and looked him in the eyes. It was all Jacob could do to hold her up.

"Abigail," he said, wondering how he was going to get her to the house without her parents finding out, "maybe we better get you sobered up."

"Did you know..." Abigail dragged out her words, "I doooo really looove you..." she giggled again. She brought her face closer to Jacob's and proceeded to kiss his lips. Jacob turned his head to stop her from kissing him. Her lips tasted very sweet and the temptation was strong. He didn't want her love like this, though, without her knowing what she was doing. If she really loved him, he wanted her to say it genuinely.

"You don't know what you are saying," Jacob said. "You don't know what you are doing."

"Jacob, don't be like that," Abigail pouted. "Don't you love me?" She continued, "I thought you loved me..." She rested her head on his chest. "I know what you think of me," she mumbled. She wasn't very cooperative, so Jacob thought carrying her would be easier. He lifted her into his muscular arms and carried her to the hired hand's house instead of taking her home.

He stood her up at the door as he lifted the latch to go inside. "You sit here while I make you a cup of coffee." He helped her sit on the chaise lounge in his sitting room next to the wood stove.

"Don't leave me, Jaky." Abigail reached out for him as he walked into the kitchen area.

"I'm right here," Jacob turned around and told her. "I will be back in a second." Abigail groaned and slouched over.

Jacob put a strong pot of coffee on the wood stove to perk. When it was ready, he got up and poured her a cup to help clear her head a little faster. "Here, drink this." Jacob helped her sit up and held the cup as she took a sip.

"That's awful." She made a funny face and turned her head away, refusing more.

"Come on," Jacob insisted. "We've got to get you back to the house before your ma and pa come looking for you." He helped her drink another sip, and she made another terrible face while swallowing.

"I don't know how you drink this stuff every day," Abigail complained.

"Well, you will remember that the next time you drink wine," he teased.

It was starting to get really late and Jacob was worried Abigail's ma and pa would come looking for her and think the worst. Abigail began to sober up and started talking like herself again. She sat up and tried to straighten her dress and apron. He watched as she felt her hair to see if it was still in place.

"Oh, my gosh," Abigail cried, "my head hurts."

Jacob laughed. "I am sure it does."

"Oh, I'm sorry, Jacob. I am an idiot," she said sheepishly. She had snuck the wine out to the barn and drank nearly half the bottle. After that she didn't remember much. "I don't know what I was thinking, or doing, for that matter."

"Ah, well, I think you got into more wine than what was served at the supper table." Jacob smiled. "Other than that, nothing happened." He wasn't going to tell her what she had said and done.

"I remember a little," she said, looking around. She finally realized she was in Jacob's quarters.

"You just fell asleep for a little while," Jacob explained.

"Oh," she said quietly, having no explanation for her actions. "Are you sure that's all that happened?" she questioned.

"Yep." He avoided eye contact as he helped her stand up. "You better get back to the house or your parents will wonder what happened," Jacob said, "and I don't think you want to have to explain this."

"You're right," Abigail said, with shame.

"Come on. I will walk you to the house."

"Well, thank you, kind sir," she smiled. She was proud to have a good friend like Jacob. "You know, Pa and Ma like you very much."

"That is why I want to get you home before they find you here," Jacob finished her sentence, "or they may not like me anymore," he joked.

They reached the back door of Abigail's house. "Well, dear lady," Jacob took off his hat and bowed down, as if to the King, "this is you." Abigail curtsied in return.

"Thank you, kind sir," she joked, then reached for her head again with her right hand. "Whoa, my head is still a little sore." She smiled. "Good night, Jacob. Thank you for saving my reputation from the public eye," she joked again. She turned toward the door, turned the knob, and went inside.

Jacob walked back to his house thinking of what had just happened. Oh, how he desired her love for real. Jacob, at the young age of seventeen, had never had a girlfriend, nor had he been with a woman in an intimate way. However, the feelings of love he felt for Abigail couldn't be mistaken. He had never known that these kinds of feelings existed until he met her. Every time he thought of the split-second kiss she had tried to give him, his whole inner body twinkled with delight. He desired her, but knew he would never have her in that way unless they were married. And that was impossible, since she was going to England to marry Patrick. Until today, Jacob had decided she would never be his, so he had tried to stop fantasizing about her and get on with his life. The night's events made this more difficult, and his desire was almost unbearable. He couldn't stop thinking about Abigail.

chapter nine

It was a beautiful Indian summer day in October. Good thing it was a gorgeous day, because that was the only thing good about it. Today was a sombre day for everyone at Goldenrod Ranch. Abigail was leaving. She was catching the CPR train from Pickets, a village ten miles south of Abbington Pickets, to start her journey to England. Her mother was going with her as far as Halifax, where Abigail would board the RMS Empress of Ireland. She would then be on her own until she reached Arlesy, Bedfordshire, where she would stay with her Aunt Gladys.

Aunt Gladys was her mother's sister, and a wonderful lady. She had never married and lived in a big, old, red brick house. Gladys cared for her parents when they became ill and passed away. She was the only one who had the room to do so. Now she had time on her hands and was happy to help Abigail until she got married.

Jacob was in the bunkhouse trying to find something in which to wrap the gift he had made for Abigail. Out of a piece of Canadian maple, he had built a small rectangular jewellery box. It had gold hinges and a little gold latch. He had carved an inlayed cross on top, and inside on the bottom he had carved a small heart with his initials in the middle: "JH." He treated the whole box with a dark brown stain and varnished it with a clear gloss coat. Jacob wanted to give Abigail a keepsake she could take with her to remember him by. Just as he was wrapping the box in a piece of linen, he heard a knock at the door.

"Jacob," Abigail's voice came from outside. "Are you in here?"

"Yes," Jacob said. "I'm coming."

"Alright. We're almost ready to leave," she said as she peeked in the door.

"You can come in, Girlie," Jacob said. "I have something for you."

Abigail walked through the doorway and closed the door behind her.

"You didn't have to do that." She blushed.

"It's nothing fancy," Jacob said. "I just made you a little something." He handed her the cloth-wrapped bundle.

"Oh, Jacob!" Abigail cried as she unwrapped the jewellery box. "It's beautiful!" she exclaimed as she looked it over. She unlatched the clasp to look inside. She saw the heart with his initials and a small piece of folded paper. She looked up at Jacob's sad face.

"I just wanted you to have something to remember me by."

Abigail gently and carefully unfolded the piece of crisp white paper. In neat handwriting, it read:

A broken heart,
not to bear,
A broken heart,
there's none to spare,
A broken heart,
for me I say,
A broken heart,
that's here to stay.

"Oh, Jacob, that's beautiful." Abigail reached up and put her arms around his neck. Jacob held her tight.

"Our friendship has meant so much to me, Abigail," Jacob whispered into her ear. "My heart is breaking as I watch you leave our little prairie world." Jacob reluctantly let go. He was trying hard not to show his emotions. "We will probably never see each other again," he continued seriously. "Just remember the time we had together."

"How could I forget that?" Abigail reached up and kissed him on the cheek. She stood back and wiped the tears from her face. She knew her feelings for Jacob were real, but had an obligation to marry Patrick. She could not go back on her word.

"We better get going," he said. "Your ma and pa are waiting."

Abigail stared at Jacob as if time were standing still for a moment. Both their hearts were breaking in two. Although they never spoke about the night she told him she loved him, and he had never really told her how he felt because he didn't want to influence her decision about marrying Patrick, he kept hoping she would change her mind on her own. However, she hadn't and he would have to let her go.

"I wish you all the best, Abigail," Jacob told her as he set his feelings aside. "I hope you are very happy with Patrick."

Jacob lifted the latch on the door. He held the door open for Abigail and followed her in. The horses and wagon were hitched and waited beside the stone house. When Jacob and Abigail reached the yard, they could see Mrs. Rodgers waiting on the seat up front. Jacob and Mr. Rodgers lifted Abigail's trunk and her other bags into the back of the wagon. Jacob helped Abigail into the back of the wagon and then hopped up and sat across from her. Mr. Rodgers stepped up into the driver's seat, held the reins, and got the horses going. It was a bit of a drive to Pickets. The train didn't leave until late afternoon, so they had time to get there without hurrying.

Later, they stood at the train station, listening to the train whistle as it approached. Big puffs of smoke came from the train's smokestack. There were a lot of people waiting at the train station. Many were on the same voyage back to England as Abigail. They had come looking for homesteading land, built their homes, had families and worked hard, but the harsh weather conditions were something many people couldn't handle. Years had passed and they were homesick for their native country, especially the women. Some women went back to England because their husbands had passed away.

The Summerfields had come in 1882 with their five sons and four daughters and founded Abbington Pickets. Mr. Summerfield created a little "Victorian Village." The village was a booming place for English settlers. He enticed many English men and women to come homestead there. Some Englishmen sent their sons over to be taught how to farm and become better gentlemen. Unfortunately, Mr. Summerfield passed away five years after coming to Canada and Abbington Pickets hadn't been the same since. His heartbroken wife, Mrs. Summerfield, packed up and went back to England.

"Well, girls," Mr. Rodgers said. "I guess we are batching it now." He meant that the two men would be bachelors while Mrs. Rodgers was gone with Abigail. He tried to make light of the sad situation and didn't want to get emotional about it. Mrs. Rodgers would be back in about ten days.

The train was stopped now, and people were coming in and out of the cars and passing them as they stood to say their good-byes.

"Goodbye, Papa," Abigail said as she shed tears. "I will miss you like crazy," she added. "I will write. I promise." She reached up and hugged her father tightly and kissed him on the cheek. She walked over to Jacob. "Good-bye, Jacob," Abigail said. She hugged him and whispered in his ear, "Jaky." She smiled and stepped back and winked at him.

"Good-bye, Girlie," Jacob said, with confusion on his face. *Did that mean she did know what she was saying the other night? Did she remember saying that she loved him?*

"Good-bye, Jacob," Mrs. Rodgers said. "You take care of Mr. Rodgers for me, please." She dabbed the corners of her eyes with a handkerchief. She said good-bye to her husband with a hug and a kiss, and gave Jacob a hug as well. She thought of him as family and it was easy for her to treat him like a son.

Jacob watched as Abigail reached for the railing and stepped up to the train steps. She disappeared inside. He watched for her through the glass windows. She sat by a window and looked out with a smile on her face. She waved at Jacob as the wheels began to turn. The train moved slowly as puffs of black smoke came from the smokestack. Jacob felt his heart being ripped from his chest at that moment. Everything seemed to move in slow motion and it all felt surreal to him.

chapter ten

The winter was a long one for Jacob. He missed Abigail terribly. Even Christmas wasn't the same without her. Every day seemed like the longest one ever. His nightmares about Lucy continued. It was as if he could never get away from them; whether he had a short nap or a long night's sleep, he would wake up in a pool of sweat.

Mrs. Rodgers was gone for ten days and then things at Goldenrod returned to normal. Well, sort of. Jacob received a letter from Abigail a month after she had left, telling him that she had reached her destination safely. Her Aunt Gladys was good to her and she had decided to go back to school before getting married.

With Abigail's absence, Jacob poured his heart into his woodwork when he wasn't working for Mr. Rodgers. Mrs. Rodgers raved about his craftsmanship and bragged to all her friends at tea. Every one of her English friends wanted to have a new tea table made by Jacob. He became quite the talk of the village. Impressed by his attention to detail, the local general store manager asked Jacob to design and produce several styles of tea table, which he offered to sell in his store.

Jacob agreed, knowing he needed to keep his mind and hands busy for the winter months.

One sunny spring Saturday, with the weather warmer than usual for the time of year, Jacob loaded his newest designs into the wagon and drove into town. Mrs. Rodgers had asked Jacob to mail a letter to Abigail while he was there.

"Well, my boy," said Mr. Adair, The General Store manager. "You've done it again. These are beautiful tables." He inspected them as they carried the tables into the store.

"Thank you, sir," Jacob said proudly.

"My customers are going to be very pleased with these," Mr. Adair added.

"I'm glad," replied Jacob.

"Three of them are already sold," Mr. Adair happily reported. "Some of the village ladies will be having a great Easter next weekend."

"I will have more finished in two weeks," Jacob assured him.

"Sounds great," Mr. Adair said as he handed Jacob an envelope with his pay for the tables.

"Thank you, sir," Jacob said. "See you in a couple weeks." Jacob nodded and left the store. He walked over to the Empire Hotel, where the post office was located. Jacob went inside and handed the letter to the postmaster. He had left the post office and started down the steps when he heard a voice behind him.

"Well, there's my good man," Charles said, happy to see his friend.

"Well, if it isn't Charles Edwards," Jacob said. "I haven't seen you in a coon's age."

"Where have you been, lad?" Charles asked, giving him a joking light punch in the arm.

"Just been busy," Jacob smiled. He didn't elaborate on his personal life with many people.

"Come on in for a drink and a game of pool." Charles put his arm around Jacob and tried to walk him in the direction of the hotel door.

Jacob had never drank, much less been in a place where people did such things. He felt a little anxious about going inside. "Well I don't know," Jacob hesitated.

"Oh, come on, lad," Charles pleaded. "Just one game."

Jacob followed him into the room with the pool table. There was a man behind the bar dressed in black. He had a moustache. Men were sitting at the bar alone. There was a big table with five men playing cards; over on the side where the pool table was, two men stood.

"Are you joining us, Charles?" one of the men at the pool table called over.

"You bet," Charles answered as he and Jacob walked over to the bartender to pay for the game. "This is Jacob," Charles introduced him to everyone. "He works for Mr. Rodgers." He pointed toward the east. "You know, the place that the Benedict boys built," he explained.

Jacob nodded to them all. He could tell that both of the men had already been drinking.

"This is Thomas and Willie," Charles introduced them. The men looked as if they could be brothers: same height, same brown hair, and same dark eyes. Their clothes looked as if they had been worn for three days straight. *A hair cut is what they need, and a good bath,* Jacob thought.

"Have you ever played pool before?" Thomas asked Jacob as he and Willie stared. Jacob felt as if he were some sort of insect that they were inspecting.

"Yes," Jacob answered coyly.

"Alrighty then, let's rack 'em up, boys," exclaimed Thomas as he placed the pool balls into the rack in the correct order. Willie brought drinks over from the bar and handed one to Jacob.

"No, thank you." Jacob shook his head.

"Come on, you ain't yella, are you?" teased Willie. "It's just a whiskey!" Jacob took the glass, sipping it slowly. He had never liked how his father acted when he drank, and he had told himself that he would never drink the stuff.

"Let's just get going," Charles piped up.

Willie flipped a coin to decide who would break first.

"I guess you're it, Charles," Willie stated.

The game started in Thomas and Willie's favour, but when it ended, Charles and Jacob had won.

"I think someone was deceiving us a little," Thomas said firmly, looking at Jacob. Jacob looked down and said nothing. "Beginner's luck then," he said as he pulled the balls from the pockets and set them back on the table. "We will see who wins the next game. Losers will be buying the drinks," Thomas said as he handed Jacob the rack. Thomas stood back, waiting to break, rubbing chalk on the tip of his cue. Jacob could sense that Thomas didn't care for him much.

"Have another drink," Willie encouraged once again, handing him a glass. Reluctantly, Jacob took the glass.

They played another game, and Jacob and Charles won again. This irritated Thomas and Willie even more, but after another round of drinks they insisted on playing again. After the fourth loss, they were fit to be tied and accused Jacob and Charles of cheating by knocking their balls into the pockets when no one was looking.

"That is ridiculous," Charles said. "You have played with me before. What are you talking about?" Jacob realized that there was no convincing these men. He was feeling light-headed and dizzy. He had never felt that way before and it seemed to loosen his tongue a little. Since he had never drank liquor before, he didn't know its potency.

Next thing he knew, a fist reached through the air and hit him on the left side of his jaw. Jacob fell backward, but quickly regained his balance. He rubbed his face with his hand. All at once Willie came lunging toward him, grabbing him and throwing him to the floor. He sat on Jacob and began punching him in the face repeatedly. Jacob managed to push him off and then punched him back. Meanwhile, Charles was fighting off Thomas. As Jacob picked up Willie and threw him across the pool table, Thomas turned around and punched Jacob in the ribs. He grabbed Thomas, picked him up, and threw him backward. He landed on the floor with a bang. Although Jacob was hardly able to stand, the men had underestimated the strength of a healthy farmhand who worked hard every day.

Jacob and Charles stumbled out of the hotel together, leaving the other two men on the floor beside the pool table. "Here." Charles handed Jacob his whiskey bottle. "This will make you feel better by morning." Charles tripped as he walked to his horse. He climbed on and the horse started to walk slowly, Charles slumped over his neck.

Jacob's head was twirling round and round as he walked about, trying to remember where he was going and what he had been doing. Stumbling and falling down too many times to count, Jacob's mind came back to the beautiful Abigail. "Oh, Abigail, why did you leave me?" Jacob hollered out loud. "I loved you, you know!" He shouted louder, as if she could hear him. He took another swallow of whisky and kept walking through the village. He remembered the many rides through the country, how her favourite thing to do was picnic in the grass under "their tree" as she called it. He remembered her picking wild flowers in the grass, and that tiger lilies were her favourite. He thought that his heart would never stop aching for her. He had a good mind to write her a letter and tell her not to marry Patrick. He loved her and wished she knew it. Better yet, he should take the first train to Halifax to catch the ship to England and go tell her in person! Yes, that was it! Jacob's mind wasn't coherent by the time he finished the last of the whisky in the bottle.

Jacob didn't remember what happened next. Hours went by. As he awakened, rubbing his head and squinting his eyes at the bright sun, he realized he wasn't at home. He heard a door slam with a loud bang that made his head hurt.

"What are you doing here?" a young woman's voice demanded.

"Excuse me, miss." Jacob struggled to sit up. "I am so sorry; I am not sure." His head was pounding in a way he had never felt before. His whole body ached with bruises and he didn't remember how he had gotten here. His shirt sleeves were ripped down the sides, revealing his muscular biceps.

"Well, what do you have to say for yourself?" A petite blonde-haired young lady stood before him with a broom in her hand. He could tell by her apron and kerchief around her head it was her cleaning day.

"I am so sorry," Jacob tried to explain. "I don't know how I got here." Realizing the state he was in, and rather embarrassed, he tucked his shirt in as he stood up. He tipped his hat to the young lady. "Forgive me." He stood there looking around, realizing that he was on someone's front porch. "I don't usually do this," he tried to explain. "Really." He stepped off the porch and started walking toward the road.

"What's your name?" the young blonde asked.

"Jacob Hudson." He stopped and turned around.

"Well, Jacob Hudson," she stated, "I just made some biscuits and you look like you could use something to eat right now." Jacob walked toward her with a shy smile on his face.

"My name is Anna," she said. "My father is the new blacksmith in town." She shook Jacob's hand. The blacksmith's shop was just across the road from the house.

"Pleased to meet you, miss," he said. Jacob took off his hat as they entered the front doorway. The house was filled with the lovely smell of freshly baked biscuits.

"Have a chair." Anna directed him toward one of the chairs at the table. She put homemade butter, jam, and biscuits in the middle of the table. She set down two plates and cutlery.

"Would you like some coffee?" she asked.

"That would be great," Jacob answered, thinking that coffee might help clear his head a little. She poured him a cup of coffee from the coffee pot keeping warm on the cookstove.

"Thank you," Jacob said as he took his first sip.

"Tell me about yourself," Anna said to Jacob.

"Not much to tell," he replied. "What about yourself?"

"It's just me and Pa," she started. "Mama died in childbirth when I was four years old."

"I am so sorry," Jacob said sympathetically.

"It's been Pa and I ever since," she continued. "We came here from Manitoba. Pa has a sister who lives south of the village, and we heard that Abbington Pickets needed a blacksmith, so we thought it was a good opportunity to be closer to family."

"I work and live at Goldenrod Ranch, east of here," Jacob told her. "I was in town yesterday delivering some tables."

"How on earth did you end up on my porch?" Anna asked.

"Well, I ran into a friend outside the Empire Hotel," Jacob remembered. "We played a couple games of pool with two guys there." He squinted his eyes as if he were trying to replay what had happened. "I had a couple drinks with them, and the next thing I knew, I was waking up on your bench." Jacob shook his head. "Thank you, miss." Jacob stood up from the table. "You have been very kind."

"Do you have to go already?" Anna jumped up and asked.

"Yes, I should be doing chores right now." Jacob picked up his hat and started to walk away. As he placed it on his head, he turned around. "Thank you again, Anna," he said as she stood at the door watching him walk away.

Jacob still needed to find the horses he had left near the hotel. Mr. Rodgers was going to be mad at him for being gone with the horses and wagon. When he reached the Empire Hotel there was no sign of his horses or his wagon. He went inside and asked the hotel owner if he had seen them.

"Sorry son, haven't seen them," he said. Jacob ran back outside and headed down the street to see if he could find the horses. Mr. Rodgers was really going to kill him now, what with missing horses and wagon. Oh, Lord, what was he going to do? He looked up and coming down the street toward Jacob was Reverend Young.

"What's the matter, Jacob?" he asked.

"Good morning, Reverend," Jacob said, out of breath from running. "I am looking for my horses and wagon."

"Sorry, son," he said, "I never saw any horses. I could help you look if you like."

"Thank you, Reverend. I will just keep looking," Jacob said as he started off running again. He spent at least an hour or so looking up and down the village for the team of horses, but to no avail. Jacob decided to face the music and walk home. As long as the journey home was, it wasn't long enough for Jacob. He didn't want to have to tell Mr. Rodgers that he had lost the horses and wagon, to boot. He was not looking forward to the conversation as he walked into the front yard and toward the house. It was dinner time, so Jacob went straight to the kitchen.

"Jacob," Mrs. Rodgers exclaimed, "you're home." Jacob could see his place was set as if they were expecting him.

"Hello." Jacob nodded sheepishly as he sat in his place. Mr. Rodgers was sitting at the head of the table in his usual spot.

"Did you have a good night?" Mr. Rodgers asked earnestly.

"Well, sir." Jacob rubbed the back of his neck with his hand, in a nervous way. "Not really," he stated plainly.

"Are you missing anything?" Mr. Rodgers asked.

"Uh, well, sir..." Jacob didn't want to say what was missing. "Well, you see..." Jacob fidgeted with the cutlery and tried hard to say what he needed to say.

"Are you alright, Jacob?" Mr. Rodgers asked. It seemed like he was slightly amused.

"Uh, yes sir," Jacob said. "You see, Mr. Rodgers, I went to Abbington Pickets to deliver tables to The General Store."

"Yes, that's what I thought you were doing," Mr. Rodgers commented.

"Well, then I saw Charles," Jacob continued, "and he asked me to play some pool at the hotel." Mr. and Mrs. Rodgers were listening very intently to Jacob's story.

"So, I played with him against a couple of guys." Jacob didn't stop. "I never drank before, honest," Jacob confirmed that detail. "Of course, Charles and I won every game," he smiled a little as he looked up at Mr. Rodgers. "The men didn't seem to like losing because next thing I knew, one of them punched me in the face." Now they were really interested in what Jacob had to say. "I don't remember what happened next, but I woke up with a pounding head on someone's porch."

"Are you okay?" Mrs. Rodgers sprang to her feet and put her arms around Jacob. "You poor boy," she said sympathetically. She then looked at Mr. Rodgers. "Now tell him," she said to him. "I think he has suffered enough."

"What are you talking about?" Jacob asked.

"Well, Myrt and Gert came home last night." Mr. Rodgers was referring to the horses and he smirked at Jacob. Jacob sighed with relief.

"I am so sorry, Mr. Rodgers," Jacob apologized. "I will never let that happen again, ever."

"You know, Jacob," Mr. Rodgers said seriously, "I believe you." He tried not to laugh, as much as he wanted to be stern about the situation. "You have been working for me for... what? Almost two years, and this is the first time something like this has happened."

"Yes, sir," Jacob concurred. "I won't let you down again."

"I know you won't, Jacob."

"Thank you for understanding, sir," Jacob said with a smile. Jacob felt so relieved that the horses had come back home and that Mr. Rodgers wasn't too upset with him. Even though the past twenty-four hours had been crazy, Jacob had to admit that it was the most entertainment he'd had in a long time. He missed Abigail so much that it felt good to forget his heartbreak, even if it was only for a few hours.

chapter eleven

It was a beautiful summer day. Robins chirped and Jacob chopped wood out at the woodshed. He heard a horse galloping toward him, and looked up to see Charles riding past the house in his direction. Jacob straightened up and greeted his friend.

"Well, long time no see," he said to Charles.

"Hello, my good lad," Charles replied as he climbed off his horse.

"What brings you out here this fine day?" Jacob asked.

"Well," Charles started, "I was thinking..." He was stalling.

"Yes?" Jacob waited for him to spit it out.

"Well, the Box Social at the church is tomorrow," Charles continued.

"And?"

"I thought you and I should go," he said all at once.

"Oh, you did, did you?" Jacob said sarcastically. "Just like the pool game?" he added with a stern look on his face.

"Ah, well..." Charles stammered. "I don't think it's the same thing," he said with a grin.

"I wouldn't think so," Jacob said plainly.

"Don't you think it's time you met some girls?" Charles asked. "Abigail's been gone close to a year now."

"And what does that have to do with anything?" Jacob asked.

"I'm just saying you can move on."

"Abigail and I were just friends," Jacob said, hiding his feelings. "Besides, she is marrying someone else."

"Well then, all the more reason to get out and meet some people," Charles added. "There are some beautiful girls here, you know," Charles said with a wink.

"Oh, alright. What time?" Jacob asked. He was tired of his friend bugging him during his working hours.

"As soon as church is over, in the church yard," Charles stated as he climbed back on his horse. "See you tomorrow!" he shouted as he rode away.

Jacob got back to his chopping, shaking his head at his friend. *He better behave himself tomorrow*, Jacob thought to himself.

The next day Jacob finished milking the cow and feeding the chickens and the horses. He had done most of his chores for that day the day before, so he could finish early and go to the Box Social.

"You look very handsome," Mrs. Rodgers said to Jacob as he saddled up his horse. He was wearing his Sunday best, a white dress shirt with new suspenders and good wool britches. The whole village and families from surrounding areas would be at church, especially since the Box Social was afterwards. Normally Jacob went to church with the Rodgers in the wagon, but since he would be having lunch with a lovely lady today, he thought it best to take his own horse. As usual, church was at 11:00 a.m. and the choir consisted of the same group of ladies. Reverend Young was his usual deep-voiced, long-winded self, conveying a great message. The young ones always seemed to get squirmy near the end of the service, which pushed the Reverend to finish sooner than he would have liked.

After church, everyone gathered outside for the Box Social. The event was to raise money to help with the upkeep of the church. All the young lads gathered around the mock stage they had built for the event. Mr. Adair, The General Store owner, acted as the auctioneer. The ladies who made the box lunches bunched together on the right-hand side of the stage. The table full of boxed lunches was on the stage beside the auctioneer. Mr. Adair stood in the centre of the stage holding the first box.

"Here is a beautiful green-covered box tied with pink ribbon. Do I have a bid of one cent?" the auctioneer started.

"Here." A gentleman put up his hand.

"Do I have two cents?"

"Over here," another gentleman held up his arm.

"Three?"

This went on until the bid was up to twenty-five cents. "Sold to the lad with the green shirt," the auctioneer said. "Green must be your favourite colour," he joked. The crowd laughed at his quip.

"Next we have this lovely blue box," he continued, "with pink flowers on the outside. Can I have one cent?"

"I will," shouted a voice.

"Two cents," shouted another voice.

That box reached thirty cents. "Now ladies and gentle-man," the auctioneer said, "remember the proceeds go to our church, so dig deep in those pockets!" He then picked up a pretty aqua-blue box decorated with pink paper flowers and tied with white ribbon. He held it up high.

"This is a beauty," the auctioneer stated. "What do you say, gents, do I hear two cents?" Well, this box sparked Jacob's interest. It looked like the prettiest box there, and something about it caught Jacob's attention.

"Here." Jacob put his hand up.

"I'll do three cents," said a voice from the back.

"Four cents," Jacob said.

"I will do ten cents," said another voice from beside Jacob.

This box seemed to have everyone's interest. Jacob figured it would go higher than the boxes which had sold already.

"Twenty-five cents." Jacob held up his hand again.

"Thirty cents," said the same voice.

"Thirty-five cents," Jacob said as he glanced beside him to see who was bidding. He recognized the young man from the Empire Hotel. Jacob stared at him as he bid again.

"Forty cents."

"Fifty cents," Jacob countered.

"Well, ladies and gentlemen," the auctioneer declared, "I do believe we are having a competition."

"Fifty-five cents," the rough-looking fellow continued.

"Seventy-five cents." Jacob didn't want to let this go. He didn't want Thomas to win. Thomas still needed a haircut and a bath, Jacob thought, and some poor girl was going to have to eat lunch with him. *Not today, son, not today,* Jacob thought to himself. It didn't matter what it was going to cost him, he was going to win this basket.

"Eighty cents," Thomas said with a smirk on his face as he looked over at Jacob.

"One dollar." The crowd all wowed at the same time.

"Wow, Mr. Hudson, the tea table business is going well for you," teased the auctioneer.

Jacob stood his ground and looked over again at Thomas to see what he was going to say. After several agonizing seconds, Thomas finally shook his head. "And...this beauty goes to Jacob," announced the auctioneer.

No one received their box until the auction was complete, so no one knew who they were having lunch with until then. There was a lot of anticipation after the auction. Jacob walked over to the stage. All the young ladies who made the boxed lunches lined up and held their boxes, so the men knew by the box they had purchased who they were having lunch with. Jacob walked up to the line-up and looked in each of the ladies' hands until he found the box he had bought. Then he looked up at the face of the lady holding it.

"It's you," was all he managed to say to the petite blonde.

"Yes, it's me." She smiled as she handed him the colourful box. "Are you disappointed?" she asked.

"Oh, gosh, no," Jacob expressed shyly. Anna looked even more beautiful than he had remembered from the morning he had woken up on her porch. Today she had on a long light pink dress with short puffed sleeves, a matching straw hat with pink trim, and a sheer sun parasol. Her blonde locks were pinned up in a puff bun. He was excited that it was her, but he tried hard not to show it.

"Where would you like to have lunch?" Jacob asked.

"Well, there is a beautiful creek down that way." She pointed south west of the church. "I have been going on quite a few walks in the afternoon and discovered it."

"Sounds great," Jacob said.

"I brought a quilt to sit on." Anna carried it folded over her arm as Jacob carried the boxed lunch. Everyone else sat on their quilts in the church yard under an evergreen tree or out in the open. It was just a little walk down a slight slope to the creek. Anna held onto her dress with one hand so she didn't trip. The blue water flowed gently. It had been a great winter for snow, so water was plentiful that spring. The creek was still running, although usually by this time of year it would be almost dried up.

"Let's sit over here," Anna directed Jacob to a small willow tree, for shade. They spread the quilt out and sat on it.

"My mama made this quilt before I was born," she explained. "I use it all the time. It makes me feel close to her."

"It's very nice," Jacob said. He didn't know what to say to her.

"I hope you like what I made," she continued. "I wasn't sure who was going to get the lunch so I just made my favourites." She smiled as she set out the napkins and food onto a tea towel, which she had laid on the quilt for a table at which to eat.

"Well, it looks delicious," Jacob said. He saw sandwiches, pickles, cookies, and iced tea set on the cloth.

"They are roasted pork sandwiches," she told Jacob. "I made the pickles myself."

"It tastes great," Jacob said, as he started eating a sandwich.

"I hope you like ginger snaps," Anna said, "because that's what the cookies are."

"Oh, I love ginger snaps," Jacob said. "My ma used to make them when I was young." He became quiet, because it made him sad to talk about his childhood.

"My aunt taught me about cooking and baking," Anna explained, "but Pa is pretty good at it too."

"I can make coffee," Jacob laughed. Anna laughed as well.

"It's so beautiful here." Anna sat back against the tree and looked up at the sky.

"It sure is," Jacob concurred as he lay on his back on the quilt.

"It's such a hot day," Anna stated. "Let's get our feet wet in the creek."

"Well..." Jacob wasn't sure how appropriate this was, since they were alone, for one, and hardly knew each other, for two. "Do you think that's such a great idea?" he asked.

"Oh, come on." Anna proceeded to take off her boots and stockings. "We will just do it for a minute." She stood up, grabbed Jacob's hands, and tugged. "Let's gooooooo," she teased as she pulled backward.

"Just a minute." Jacob laughed as he pulled his hands away. "Don't you think I should take my boots off too?"

"Oh, alright, if you insist," Anna said sarcastically with a laugh.

The creek felt cool but delicious on Jacob's feet, although he felt a little anxious, since showing your feet wasn't a very acceptable thing to do with a girl, especially one you weren't actually courting or engaged to.

Anna walked with one foot in front of the other in front of Jacob. She held her dress up with her left arm, which made her unbalanced.

"Careful not to slip," Jacob said when she almost lost her footing. "Here, take my hand." Jacob worried she would fall. Anna turned around and grabbed his hand with her right one. They interlocked their fingers together tightly.

The water flowed along past their ankles as they walked on the bottom of the creek. The soggy slippery grass felt smooth on the bottoms of their feet.

All in an instant Anna slipped. Even though she was holding Jacob's hand firmly, with a big splash down she went. She landed on her backside with her two feet in the air. She took Jacob with her, because she was holding onto his hand. Jacob fell over frontward, right in front of where Anna landed, down on his knees.

Anna burst out laughing as she sat there in the cool water with Jacob at her feet. Jacob looked up at Anna. Seeing her with her hair drenched and water dripping down her face was such a sight that he couldn't possibly keep from laughing as well.

"Oh, my goodness," Anna wailed with her head tipped back. She was laughing so hard that tears streamed down her face.

"Well, look at us." Jacob was still chuckling. "I bet we are a sight." He stood up while holding Anna's hand for stability, then he helped her to her feet. "I think we better call this a day," Jacob said as they walked carefully out of the creek and toward the quilt.

"You can't get my quilt wet," she told Jacob. "Just carefully pick it up and we will carry it to the house."

"Alright." He remembered what the quilt meant to her.

They gathered their boots, stockings and lunch things together and started walking toward Anna's house. "Well, it's been an exciting day," Jacob said to Anna as they stood on her porch in front of the door. "Oh, here." He handed the quilt to her. "Don't forget this."

"Thank you, Jacob Hudson."

"No, thank you, Miss Anna." Jacob couldn't help but laugh. "I better go find my horse and get out of these wet clothes."

"Me too." Anna unlatched the door and went inside.

Jacob walked to the church, just east of Anna's house, past the flour mill and the water well. It was a nice ride home. In the heat of the day the breeze blowing through his cool, wet clothes felt good.

Jacob didn't know how he felt about Anna. He still had incredibly strong feelings for a woman he could never have. He felt he was betraying himself if he even thought of another woman the way he had thought of Abigail.

chapter twelve

It was harvest time once again, and it was a sad time for Jacob. It was almost a year ago that Abigail had told him she loved him. Even though she was under the influence of wine, the experience still came to mind and made him yearn for her. Maybe she really did have feelings for him? He guessed he would never truly know. In all the letters they had exchanged over the previous twelve months, there were brief mentions of weather and a few pieces of news, but never anything intimate or private. There is something to be said about not getting what you can't have; it makes you want it all the more. Abigail had left a hole in Jacob's soul that could never be filled.

Jacob saw Anna a couple of times after the Box Social, and in church every Sunday. Soon the summer dwindled and Goldenrod Ranch started getting busier with the beginning of harvest season. There was no time to be creating new tables, and there wasn't much need to go to the village as often. They only made the trip for parts needed for repairs and things of that nature.

On the last day of harvest, Mr. Rodgers toasted to another great year. "Are you going to the Harvester's Ball at the Howards'?" Mrs. Rodgers asked Jacob after supper. Jacob looked at her with surprise. "Well. I thought maybe you would ask that nice girl you had lunch with at the Box Social this summer." She looked at him with her head half turned, as if she was worried what the answer would be.

"I don't know," Jacob hesitated. "I didn't really think I would be going, so I never gave it any thought."

"Well, you never do anything exciting," she insisted, "and Mr. Rodgers and I are going. It will be fun." Jacob was hesitant because even though he thought Anna was a wonderful lady, his heart belonged to another. It wouldn't be fair to Anna if he made her believe he could be more than a friend.

"I will consider it," Jacob said. He was thinking it would be neat to see the grand house. The Howards lived in a big house a mile and a half southwest of Abbington Pickets. It had originally been built by a man named Daniel Mathewson, who had brought his family from England. He had five boys and five girls. He was a well-known marine architect. On the prairies he built a unique house; it was two stories high, constructed like a ship. It was a big square house painted white. The interior of the twenty-two room house included two staircases, one on each side of the house. The beautifully carved railing encased the opening to the top floor balcony on all four sides. People could look down over the railing from upstairs to the centre of the main floor to view the dance floor.

There was also a big kitchen with a water pump installed. Not many people had that luxury on the prairies. There was a billiard room for the men to relax in and have their cigars, and a grand dining room for social events. Smaller rooms included a sitting room and a photography room. When Mr. Mathewson died, Mrs. Mathewson and two of her girls moved to Victoria, British Columbia. Their other children married locals and scattered around the area. The house was bought by the Howards. Their family wasn't as big as the Mathewsons', but they utilized the space, as they had many relatives who visited often.

The sound of his knocking was all he could hear as Jacob stood outside Anna's front door. The door opened. "Well, if it isn't Mr. Jacob Hudson." Anna stood in the doorway and smiled.

"Hello Anna," Jacob said, as he took off his hat and held it in his hands in front of him. "How are you this fine afternoon?" The weather was still warm and sunny, even though it was mid-October.

"I am pretty good, and you?" She stood there holding the door open. Anna had on a long blue dress covered with her everyday apron. Her hair was neatly pinned in a bun. It was obvious that she had been baking. Jacob could see a streak of flour across her forehead. He smiled to himself.

"I am doing alright," Jacob said as he shuffled from foot to foot. He was waiting for the right moment to ask his question.

"So, what brings you all the way into Abbington?" she asked.

"Ah, um, well," Jacob stammered. "I was wondering," he added as he looked down at his feet.

"Yes?" She looked at him, wide-eyed, and leaned forward as if to drag it out of him.

"I was wondering..." he repeated.

"Yes, you said that," she laughed.

"I was wondering if you would like to..." he started to say really fast, "...if you would like to go to the Harvester's Ball at the Howards'?" Jacob held his breath waiting for her answer.

"Sure," Anna replied quickly. "Sounds like fun."

"It's this Saturday," he added. "I'll pick you up at six-thirty."

"I will be here with bells on," Anna said with delight.

"Sounds great." Jacob smiled. He stepped back and said awkwardly, "Thank you." He nodded and continued to walk backward as he put his hat back on. Then he turned around and walked toward his horse. *Well, Mrs. Rodgers, I took your advice,* Jacob thought to himself, *hope you're happy.* He smiled to himself as he rode home.

Saturday came quickly. The farm work got done faster than usual. Everyone was anxious to get ready for the ball. Once again Jacob put on his Sunday best. Since there was only one wagon at the ranch, Mr. and Mrs. Rodgers were with Jacob when he picked up Anna. There were other families riding out to the Howards' and the trail was busy that evening. The sky was dark and the air had cooled off considerably. They had packed blankets to cover up themselves on the ride home.

They arrived at the Howards' around seven-thirty that evening. Most of Abbington Pickets was there. The women wore their best dresses and the men their best suits for the occasion. Mr. Rodgers pulled the wagon right up to the front door of the beautiful white house to let the women off. Then he and Jacob drove the wagon to the stables behind the house, where they would tie the horses for the evening.

As soon as the front door opened, they heard the sound of fiddle music above many people talking at once. The rumours were correct. The house was all everyone said it would be and then some. "Good evening," Mr. and Mrs. Howards greeted them as they entered through the double doors. There in front of them, on each side of the entrance, were the two grand staircases with beautiful hand-carved railings. Jacob walked beside Anna, behind Mr. and Mrs. Rodgers, through the arch between the staircases which led into the grand room. *What a sight,* Jacob thought to himself. The interior structure was similar to the Rodgers', with good reason, as Mr. Mathewson had designed both houses.

There were familiar faces amongst the men and women dancing in the middle of the dance floor. They were dancing to "When the Harvest Days Are Over, Jessie Dear," by a local band. Some of the local bachelors stood around the fireplace with their drinks, visiting, while some of the women sat in the chairs that were lined up along the walls around the room. Everyone was happy and enjoying the fun. There was delicious food on a beautifully decorated table in the corner of the room. The punch bowl was filled with a tasty fruity-flavoured beverage.

"Jacob, my boy!" A loud voice came from across the room. Jacob turned to see who it was. His red-headed friend came hustling over to see him. Charles was dressed in a brown wool suit complete with a top hat. When he reached Jacob, he slapped him on the back and shook his hand. "Who's this young lady?" Charles smiled with a wink.

"This is Anna," Jacob introduced the two of them. "Anna, this is my friend Charles. We went to school together."

"Pleased to meet you," Anna said, putting her hand out to Charles. He held her hand and gently kissed the back of it. Charles was not the gentleman he was pretending to be, but every now and again he tried to impress the ladies.

"You remember Mr. and Mrs. Rodgers, don't you?" Jacob asked as he directed Charles toward them.

"Of course," Charles said, as he shook Mr. Rodgers's hand and kissed Mrs. Rodgers's hand and made her blush.

"Jacob." Mrs. Rodgers looked at him and said, "We are going to mingle. We will see you later, when it's time to leave."

"Sounds good, Mrs. Rodgers," Jacob answered her.

"Come with me, laddie." Charles pulled Jacob's arm. "Do you mind if I steal him for a quick moment, Anna?" He pulled Jacob toward the front entrance of the house.

"What's the matter?" Jacob asked. "Why were you so rude to Anna back there?"

"Listen, my boy." Charles's face was serious now. "I just want to warn you." Now he was starting to scare Jacob a little.

"What are you talking about?" Jacob insisted.

"When I got here, I saw your mother and father." Charles had a sympathetic look on his face. Charles knew the situation between Jacob and his father. Jacob felt excited in one moment because he would get to see his ma again, but he felt his heart drop thinking of meeting his father.

"Thanks, Charles," Jacob said. "I'll be okay, but thanks for thinking of me." Jacob gave him the best smile he could muster. "I better get back to Anna," he said as he started back to the ballroom. "She doesn't know many people. It will be a little awkward for her." When he got back to where he had left her, he found that she was gone. A few minutes later he spotted her dancing with someone. *Now who is she dancing with?* Jacob wondered. At that moment, the couple spun around and he saw that it was his older brother, Andrew. When the song was over and they had finished their dance, they came over to Jacob.

"Well, hello little brother," Andrew said. "I haven't seen you since forever and a day." He shook Jacob's hand and they hugged briefly. Jacob was delighted to see one of his family members and happy to see how well he looked. Andrew was right; it had been a very long time since he had last seen him.

In fact, it was the day the family cut wood together over two years ago.

"Wow. It's good to see you, Andrew." Jacob smiled from ear to ear.

"You still being a carpenter?" Andrew asked.

"You bet," Jacob said. "When I'm not working at the ranch."

"Are you making any money at it?"

"Well, I am selling to Mr. Adair." Jacob told him.

"The General Store owner?" Andrew asked. Jacob nodded.

"That's fantastic. Good for you, brother."

"How's Mama?" Jacob asked his brother.

"She misses you, Jacob," his brother said sadly.

"Well, Pa won't let me come to the house," he explained. "Not since I left."

"Sarah is getting married," Andrew stated.

"That's wonderful," Jacob said. He was happy for her, but sad inside because he would miss the wedding.

"Jane is a great help to Mama," Andrew continued. "She will die an old maid." They laughed at the joke.

"What's Peter busy at?" asked Jacob.

"Same as always," Andrew told him. "We are farming like we have been. We help Pa out when we can," he continued. "Pa has aged a lot since you left, Jacob. He doesn't look so good."

Jacob held his head down, feeling shame, but not guilt. He knew one way or another that he had little choice but to leave his father. The secret they held together, yet apart, kept them in an internal war that Jacob didn't think would ever be resolved.

"You know what?" Andrew said with excitement in his voice. "Peter is courting someone." Andrew grinned from ear to ear.

"No way, really?" Jacob was surprised. Peter never seemed to be interested in girls. All he wanted to do was work, work, and more work.

"You will never guess who," Andrew teased.

"Who?"

"Missy Hamilton."

"Good for him. I thought he would end up the oldest bachelor ever to live." They both laughed.

"Hey, are you going to vote on Monday?" Andrew asked. "Now that you're old enough!" He laughed at his own little joke.

"You bet," Jacob said. "Mr. Rodgers and I are planning on going together."

"Well, Prime Minister Laurier is doing such a great job," Andrew pointed out, "I hope he gets in again."

"Me too," Jacob agreed, "and Mr. Rodgers thinks so too."

"Look at you," Andrew touched Jacob's shoulder to feel his suit. "All grown up, and looking smart."

"Yep." Jacob felt embarrassed by his comment and blushed a little. "You wash up pretty good yourself." Jacob laughed and his brother appeared pleased with himself as well. All joking aside, it felt so good to have a conversation with his brother and catch up on some of the family news.

"So, how did you meet this raving beauty?" Andrew teased again as he looked at Anna.

"Don't ask." Jacob smiled as he remembered the day on Anna's porch. Anna blushed as she also recalled the moment when she first saw Jacob.

"Are you here with anyone?" Jacob asked his brother.

"Sadly, no," Andrew smirked, "I came with Pa and Ma." He looked around the room to see if he could spot them. "I could keep Pa entertained," Andrew suggested, "while you talk to Ma."

"I don't know," Jacob hesitated. "Last time wasn't exactly fun."

"Ma would love to see you."

"I know but I don't think it's a great idea."

"Jacob," Anna interrupted, gently touching his arm, "maybe you should."

Jacob could see his mother across the room, talking with Mrs. Ford. Her face had aged ten years in the last two.

"Oh, all right," Jacob said reluctantly. However, deep down he was happy to go talk to her. He just didn't want to incur the wrath of his father.

Jacob and Anna walked around the dance floor while the music played. Andrew did what he had said he would and kept his father occupied.

"Good evening, Mama." Jacob walked up behind his mother as she was visiting.

"Oh, my goodness." His mother turned around with excitement. She held her hands over her mouth in disbelief. Jacob gently hugged his mother and kissed her cheek. He could feel her frailty when he touched her. Even her hair had gone a little grey since he had seen her last.

"How are you keeping, Mama?" Jacob asked.

"I am good, my son," she told him. "How about you? I didn't know you were going to be here." She held his hand tightly, as if never to let go.

"I want you to meet a friend of mine, Mama," Jacob said as he turned to Anna. "This is Anna. Anna, this is my mama."

"It's a pleasure, ma'am." Anna put her hand out to greet Mrs. Hudson.

"Oh, you are a pretty little thing." His mama held on to her hand.

"Thank you." Anna blushed shyly and shifted her feet from side to side with her head down.

"She sure is," Jacob beamed.

"Have you seen your father?" his mother asked.

"No, I haven't," Jacob said quietly. He hugged her again. "Good-bye Mama, I am going to take this lovely lady for a dance." He took Anna by the hand and led her out onto the dance floor.

The band played a slow-paced song, and Jacob, who had never really danced before, stepped in time to the music. He held Anna close to him, with his arm around her waist and his hand at her back. His other hand held hers in the air in the usual dancing manner. Jacob felt like they were the only ones in the room, though in fact the room was full of neighbours and friends. He could smell the perfume that Anna was wearing. It reminded him of the sweet smell of Abigail. It made him long for Abigail, but he was also quite intrigued by Anna, for she had a different disposition than Abigail. For the moment, time stood still. Jacob's face was so very close to Anna's. His heart raced with excitement as they danced to the rhythm of the music.

"What are you thinking?" Anna whispered.

"How I love the smell of you." Jacob stared into Anna's blue eyes. Anna smiled and blushed. She blushed easily, as she had such a fair complexion.

The music stopped and the dancers scattered to wait for the next set. "Ready for some punch?" Jacob asked Anna.

"Sounds great. I am very thirsty," she replied. They walked over to the refreshment table in the corner.

"Excuse me, ladies and gentleman," a loud deep voice echoed from above. Everyone looked up to see Mr. Howards, on the second-floor balcony, looking down at the room full of people.

"Can I have everyone's attention?" he continued. "We are having such a wonderful time here, aren't we?" Everyone in the room cheered in agreement. "As you all know, this is the Harvesters' Ball, where we celebrate the completion of the harvest." Everyone stood still, intently listening to Mr. Howards. "I would love to tell you to keep dancing and being merry," he said, "but in fact I can't."

Everyone in the room went "Ahhhh..."

"It appears that there is a terrible winter storm headed this way," he explained. With that, everyone started to scurry around, finding their coats and hats. The men went rushing outside to gather horses and wagons. Everyone knew that a winter storm in the prairies could hit at any moment, anywhere from October to April.

"Wait here, Anna," Jacob told her. "I will go with Mr. Rodgers and get the wagon." Anna nodded and waited with Mrs. Rodgers.

Outside, the snowflakes were already floating in the air. The wind was starting to blow and was bound to get worse. Jacob and Mr. Rodgers pulled the wagon up close to the house. There were many wagons already lined up, picking up the ladies. The men rushed to get the women into their wagons. Jacob hurried back into the house to give his regards to the hosts, and to find Anna and Mrs. Rodgers.

"Good-bye, Mr. Howards," he said as he shook his hand. "Mrs. Howards." Jacob tipped his hat. He then helped the ladies get into the wagon. It was a good thing Jacob and Mr. Rodgers had decided to put the cover on the wagon the previous week. The women covered their laps with the blankets they had packed.

"Hee-ya." Mr. Rodgers got the horses going. As they drove the wagon slowly past the house, Jacob saw his pa getting his horse and wagon ready. His father looked up from his horse at the very moment they passed by. Jacob's eyes met his father's. It seemed as if they were moving in slow motion. Jacob's heart was beating almost out of his chest. He felt fear as if he was still a small boy. He saw guilt written all over his father's face. Guilt from the death of Lucy. Jacob lifted his hand and waved to him, and no sooner did he wave than his father looked away. It was as if Jacob was invisible. Jacob couldn't believe that any person, and a God-fearing person at that, could have so much hatred in his heart for another human being. He focused on the thought that he was grateful for the opportunity to visit with his mother.

The wind started to pick up and the snow got heavier. It made it hard on the men driving because they weren't as protected as the women were. Jacob took over driving the horses while Mr. Rodgers took a break to warm up in the back of the wagon with the ladies. Jacob wrapped an extra blanket around himself to keep warm. The snow was coming down with extreme force now. The ride from the Howards' to the Rodgers' was four and a half miles. On a good day it would take two hours, but these weather conditions would slow them down considerably.

Jacob could see that the horses were struggling through the snow, but he knew they couldn't stop. The snow piled on top of their backs like blankets. They kept putting their heads down because of the blinding snow, but Jacob pushed them on. He vaguely saw a landmark at the side of the trail, so now he knew exactly where he was. Jacob felt relieved. He had been starting to think that he was lost. However, they were still two hours from home.

"Son," Mr. Rodgers yelled from the back so Jacob could hear him, "I'll trade places with you now."

"Okay," Jacob hollered back. "I know where we are, just at the Griffin Rock." Mr. Rodgers nodded. It was hard to talk over the bellowing song of the wind with the snow stinging their faces. Jacob climbed out of the driver's seat, still holding the reins and looking in the direction they were going, while Mr. Rodgers climbed up in his spot. He tried not to disturb the pattern of their positions or startle the horses. He took the reins from Jacob and Jacob crawled out of the way and into the back. His hands were very cold, and the riding gloves he was wearing were thin, but at least they were some protection from the wind. Mrs. Rodgers, Anna, and Jacob huddled together to keep warm.

"We shouldn't have left the Howards'," Mrs. Rodgers said. "No one should have left. The house was big enough that everyone would have made do." She was shivering and her lips were quivering, so badly that her speech slurred.

"It's all right, Mrs. Rodgers." Jacob held her hands in his. "We will be at Anna's soon."

"Yes, and you all can stay at our house," Anna added. "It isn't safe out here. We need to stay together." Jacob looked at Mr. Rodgers to make sure he was doing all right. They felt the wagon turning. Jacob thought they must be almost at Abbington Pickets.

"See there," Jacob reassured her, "we are almost to Anna's."

"Who would have expected weather like this to happen so fast?" Mrs. Rodgers said. "Why it was just over a week ago we were celebrating Thanksgiving in the great outdoors."

"Here in the prairies," Jacob explained, "if you don't like the weather, wait five minutes and it will change." He tried to keep everyone in good spirits even though he knew how serious their situation was. It seemed like forever until they felt the wagon slowing down.

"We must be at Anna's," Jacob said as he bent to climb to the front. Mr. Rodgers had icicles hanging from his moustache and eyebrows. He looked frozen to the bone. Jacob hopped off the wagon and helped everyone off. The ladies carried the blankets. When they reached the door, it burst open. There was a large man with a full beard and moustache standing in the doorway.

"Pa!" Anna exclaimed.

"Oh, my Anna," her father said. "I have been worried sick about you." He looked at them all standing frozen near the door. "Come in, come in," he said as he moved out of the way so they could walk through the doorway.

"The heat feels wonderful," Mr. Rodgers said as he walked over to the middle of the room where the cookstove stood heating the one-room house. Anna's father started putting on his coat and boots.

"I will go put the horses in the barn," he said. "You stay here and keep warm."

"Thank you, sir," Jacob said gratefully. "We need a place to stay until this storm blows over."

"Of course, lad," Anna's father said. "Our home is your home." He opened the door and the wind blew in a gust of snow. Everyone felt the draft of cold air. Fifteen minutes had gone by when the door burst open again and in came Anna's father. He took off his coat and boots at the door and walked over to the stove. He rubbed his hands together, trying to get warm quickly.

"Pa, this is Mr. and Mrs. Rodgers," Anna introduced them, "and this is Jacob."

"It's a pleasure," her father said as he nodded to each of them and shook Jacob's and Mr. Rodgers's hands.

"No one saw this storm coming this morning," he said.

"I have never seen anything like it," Mr. Rodgers said.

"About ten years ago," Jacob started, "there was a blizzard that took the life of one person and almost that of another."

"How terrible," Anna said, with sadness in her voice.

"Oh, my," Mrs. Rodgers said, putting her hand over her mouth.

"A husband and wife were coming home from Kingston," Jacob started to tell the story. "They stopped off at the stopping house in the middle of the storm. The folks there tried to talk them into staying until the storm cleared, but the couple figured that since they were not far from home they would persevere." Jacob shook his head. "The next day one of neighbours found their wagon upside down and burnt."

"Oh, no." Both ladies gasped, waiting to hear the rest of the story.

"Apparently the husband had lit the wagon on fire to keep them warm. When the fire burnt out, they proceeded on foot. After a little way the lady couldn't go any further, so he carried her." Everyone was very quiet, waiting to hear the outcome of the story. "He carried her so far and then he couldn't go any further. They found them the next day. The Mrs. had frozen to death, but he was still alive."

"I can't believe it," Anna said. "Why didn't they just stay put when they had the chance?"

"What happened to the husband?" Mrs. Rodgers asked.

"He had severe frost bite. Both legs had to be amputated and his face was so disfigured that he was unrecognizable."

They sat quietly around the warm cookstove in silence, shocked by what they had heard. They all knew that it could have been them had they not arrived at Anna's when they did.

"Better put a candle in the window," Jacob suggested. "That way, if there is someone lost in the storm, they might see it and know we are here."

"Great idea, lad," Mr. Rodgers said. Anna got up from her chair and rummaged through the drawers in the kitchen to look for candles.

"Here," she said, holding a few in her hand, "I found some." She placed one in a candleholder, lit it with a wooden match, and set it in the window.

"Lord, if anyone is out there, please let them see this light," Anna whispered as the flame burned.

"They will," Jacob said as he walked up behind her to reassure her. Again, Jacob could smell Anna's perfume and it made him feel wonderful inside. He never wanted to lose that feeling, as he had with Abigail. He didn't want to get hurt again. He wanted to shield his feelings from ever being exposed.

Anna and Mrs. Rodgers made beds for Jacob and Mr. Rodgers on the floor and then everyone settled in for the night. It felt good to be safe, warm, and out of the cold.

Anna and Mrs. Rodgers shared the big bed. Anna's father slept on the smaller bed in the living room, where Anna usually slept. The night wasn't a quiet one. The wind blew strong and mighty. It snowed so much that it built up on the window sill and almost covered half the window. Anna's father got up every few hours to fill the stove so the house would stay warm.

"Nooooooooo!" Jacob awoke. He sat straight up, shaking. Once again, his terrible nightmare had come to haunt him.

"Are you all right, son?" Mr. Rodgers sat up next to him.

"Yes sir," Jacob said. He was wide awake now, with sweat trickling down his forehead. He could feel the coolness of his damp shirt. "Just a dream," he said, not wanting to alarm him.

"I think that was more than a dream," Mr. Rodgers persisted. "Do you have them often?" he asked.

"No," Jacob said. He didn't feel good about lying to Mr. Rodgers, but he couldn't explain that he always had horrible dreams of his father killing his baby sister. Jacob slid down into his bed on the floor, pulled the covers back over his chest, and pretended to go back to sleep. Mr. Rodgers lay back down and soon started snoring. Jacob hoped that he would not mention it in front of anyone tomorrow.

Bang, bang, bang. The sound echoed throughout the one-room house. Jacob was closest to the door; he got up quickly and opened it. A gust of wind pushed snow inside onto the floor. A man stood, wrapped from head to toe in clothing. Snow was piled on top of his hat and he had icicles hanging from his moustache.

"Oh, my gosh!" Jacob grabbed the man's arm and pulled at him, helping him step inside the house. "Come in, quickly."

By this time Anna's father was standing near the doorway. "Yes, please come in," he said. They helped the man take his outside clothes and boots off to warm up faster. Neither of them recognized him. He was a young man with short dark brown hair, with a tidy handlebar moustache. He was shivering so much that he was unable to speak. Mr. Rodgers pushed a chair up close to the wood stove and Jacob and Anna's father helped the stranger walk over to it. Mrs. Rodgers folded a quilt in half and placed it around his shoulders. Anna put the kettle on the stove to make some coffee to warm him up.

"Are you all right?" Jacob knelt down to be closer to the unknown gentleman. The drifter nodded his head. His teeth were chattering so much that he was unable to speak.

"It's all right son, we can talk later," Anna's father convinced him and he nodded.

Outside it was still snowing and blowing. Mr. Rodgers and Anna's father went outside to feed and check on the horses. Anna and Mrs. Rodgers made scrambled eggs, bacon, and biscuits for breakfast. It was apparent that no one would be going anywhere until the blizzard let up. Jacob hauled in more wood for the cookstove. Meanwhile, the stranger had warmed up and was able to tell his story.

"I saw the light in the window," he explained to everyone over breakfast. Jacob glanced at Anna, as if to say, *See, I told you it would work*. Anna blushed and smiled.

"Where are you from, lad?" Mr. Rodgers asked.

"I came from Arlsley, England, sir," the young man said. You could tell by his manners that he grew up in a good family. Jacob took a liking to the young lad right away.

"Well, aren't you a little far away from home?" Jacob joked.

"I came to Canada for a job," he explained. "By the way, my name is Bert. Bert Hibbert." He put his hand out and shook the men's hands. He nodded to the ladies. "It's a pleasure to meet you. I sailed on the Empress of Ireland to Ontario, and then caught the train to Kingston. I bought a horse there and rode until the storm hit. I don't know what would have happened if I hadn't seen the light in the window." He shook his head with a sad look on his face. "My bride-to-be is going to join me as soon as I find work and save enough money to send for her." His face lit up as soon as he spoke of his fiancé.

"That's so romantic," Anna said quietly.

"So, you don't know where you were headed?" Anna's father asked.

"I was told in Kingston that Abbington Pickets was a great place to find work," he explained. "No one explained that winter came without a moment's notice." He smiled.

"Well, it is an interesting climate here," Mr. Rodgers said, as they too were from England. "You will get used to it, and you will learn from it as well." Everyone laughed.

"God works in mysterious ways," Mrs. Rodgers expressed.

"You are right," Bert said. "Thank the Lord I found you fine folks. I am truly blessed," he continued. "Alice will find this an amazing story when I write to her." There was something about Bert that everyone was drawn to. He had charisma in the way that he spoke. He was also a kind and gentle soul.

Another day passed before there was a break in the weather. Before leaving Anna's house, Jacob took Bert to see the village and showed him the Empire Hotel. He would stay there until he found work. Mr. Rodgers hitched up the horses and Mrs. Rodgers helped Anna with the dishes from their early breakfast. When Jacob got back from the hotel, he wanted to say good-bye to Anna, but there was little privacy in the one-room house. All they had time for was a brief, "good-bye, so long," at the door along with everyone else. Jacob's eyes met Anna's and both knew that they wanted to say more.

"Boy, there will be a lot of snow to shovel when we get home," Jacob said as they drove into their lane. The horses had a tough time pulling the wagon with all the snow. After each mile, they stopped to give the horses a rest. "I guess we will be digging out the sleigh and putting the wagon away," he chuckled. *But then you never know, the snow may leave and it could be fall again for a while,* he thought to himself.

chapter thirteen

It turned out that Jacob was wrong. Winter came in full force that year and there was hardly a day it didn't snow. If it didn't snow during the day, it snowed during the night. It was a tough winter for everyone. It was harder to feed the cattle and horses and more difficult to get to the village for supplies. Usually, one person would venture into town and get the things needed and come home promptly, and it would be a while before they would go again.

Jacob had been crafting more tables to sell at The General Store, but it was difficult to get them to Mr. Adair. A couple of times, when it was Jacob's turn to go into Abbington Pickets, he stopped and had tea and biscuits with Anna. These were the only times he could see her, besides church on Sunday, but it was becoming impossible to go to church every Sunday, due to the amount of snow. It snowed so much in December that the snow piled up to the roof of the barn.

Today was a beautiful sunny day in February, and Jacob had planned a trip into town despite the amount of snow. He got up extra early to do his chores so that he could be home by dark. He carefully packed his tables into the sleigh to take them to Mr. Adair. He would also pick up flour from the mill while he was in town, for Mrs. Rodgers.

The three-mile ride took twice the time it usually did, but Jacob was dressed warmly for the longer ride. He wore a hat with ear muffs and thick leather gloves. He also had extra blankets for his legs. He reached the village before dinner time and first went to see Mr. Adair at The General Store to unload the sleigh.

"You have been hard at it, I see," exclaimed Mr. Adair. "Looks very fine, very fine." He inspected each table as he helped carry them into the store. "Come in, Jacob," Mr. Adair said to Jacob. "I have something I want to speak to you about."

"I don't have a lot of time, sir," Jacob replied, "but I can stop for a moment." He followed Mr. Adair into his office at the back of the store. It was a tidy little room with a desk and two chairs. There were books on shelves on the wall behind the desk and extra merchandise piled on shelves at the other side of the room.

"Sit down, lad." He directed Jacob to the chair. Jacob sat in front the desk while Mr. Adair sat across from him behind the desk. "Have you given any thought," he started out, "to going into business for yourself?" He tipped his chair as he leaned backward with his fingers locked behind his head.

"No, sir," Jacob said. "Not really." He was confused; Mr. Adair's question seemed to come out of the blue.

"You have a gift," Mr. Adair said kindly. "You should consider opening a little shop, where you could build your tables, and even more, and then have a little store in the front to sell them."

"Is there really money in this?" Jacob asked.

"There sure is," Mr. Adair replied. "I don't think you realize how talented you really are."

Jacob thought that anyone could build a table. Anyone could be a craftsman. He didn't think that what he was doing was anything special. He loved to build things, that was for sure, but he didn't really think he could make a living at something he loved. *It doesn't work like that, does it? Don't you have to work your fingers to the bone before you can make a dollar?*

"I guess I don't, sir," Jacob answered.

"Well, I have a suggestion for you," Mr. Adair started to explain. "The Empire Hotel, next door, has a space for rent. It's big enough for a workshop and a small store to display your tables."

"Hmm." Jacob didn't know what to think.

"There is even a small room in the back which could be used for living space, you know, until you grow bigger."

"I don't know," Jacob said.

"I could help you get started. I could advertise your new store and send you customers who are interested in carpentry work. You may even get custom work."

"I'm very grateful for your idea, Mr. Adair," Jacob said. "Really, I don't know. I will have to talk to Mr. Rodgers." Jacob stood up with his hat in his hand.

"Think about it, Jacob," Mr. Adair said. "Come see me when you decide."

"Thank you, sir." Jacob turned and walked out the doorway, putting his hat back on. It was a lot to think about. Mr. and Mrs. Rodgers had been so good to him, but on the other hand, it had been painful staying at Goldenrod without Abigail. The change might be a good thing. He had saved quite a bit of money since he had started working for Mr. Rodgers. It was a lot to mull over.

Jacob climbed on the sleigh and drove the horses over to the flour mill. He would have just enough time for a visit with Anna before going back home before dark.

Jacob knocked on Anna's door. It was only a moment before the door swung open. There stood Anna with a big smile on her face. Her cheeks were pink and her apron was slightly soiled.

"Jacob!" Anna exclaimed. "Come on in. I just made some tea and biscuits." She wiped her hands on her apron and moved away from the door. Jacob took off his hat as he entered the house.

"Thank you, miss," Jacob joked with her.

"I was hoping you would come see me soon," Anna began. "I thought it was a beautiful day today and now this makes it a beautiful, wonderful, lovely day." She giggled.

"It is indeed a beautiful day," Jacob smiled, "with beauty all around." He winked at Anna.

"Oh, stop." Anna blushed. "You're too much."

"Ah, but I do know what I'm talking about," Jacob assured her. He grabbed Anna by the hand and pulled her toward him. She spun around to face him and giggled. "I have missed that laugh," Jacob said. This made her giggle even more.

"You are such a joker, Jacob Hudson," Anna informed him.

"No way," Jacob smiled. "I tell nothing but the truth."

"I better serve the tea," Anna said. "Come sit down." She pulled him to the table.

Jacob pulled the chair out for Anna to sit down. "Ladies first," he said to her.

"Oh, Jacob. I have to pour tea and get the biscuits," Anna argued.

"I will pour the tea," Jacob insisted. "I will get the biscuits. You sit down." He presented the chair as if it was the Queen's throne. Anna gave in and sat down. Jacob picked up the tea towel lying on the table and tucked the short end of it in the front of his trousers as if it were an apron. Then he picked up the teapot and poured tea into the cup in front of Anna before pouring his own. He took the basket of biscuits from the countertop and placed them in the middle of the table, along with the butter and jam sitting on the cupboard.

"You are a good waiter, Mr. Ahhhh... What was your name again?" Anna played along with Jacob's game.

"Monsieur Hudson, miss." Jacob tried to keep a straight face.

Anna laughed. "You're too funny." She couldn't stop laughing at the expression on Jacob's face while he served the biscuits and pretended he was a French waiter. Jacob sat down to enjoy Anna's biscuits and her company. Time was ticking and he needed to get going soon. He still had to stop at the post office before he left Abbington, to mail Mrs. Rodgers's letter.

"It was so good to see you, Jacob," Anna said to him as he put on his jacket to get ready to weather the cold waiting for him outside.

"I thought I would drop by, since it's been such a wicked winter," he said. "We've been cooped up at Goldenrod without seeing anyone for weeks."

"I know what you mean," Anna agreed. "Pa is the only person I see, unless I go to the post office. Spring can't come soon enough." She sighed.

"I hear you." Jacob stood at the door restlessly. He wanted to touch Anna, but he knew it wasn't proper to touch a lady, let alone kiss her, especially when no one else was in the house. His desire to kiss her lips was strong, and he wanted to pull her close to him and hug her tightly before he left, but he didn't. "Thank you for the tea and biscuits." Jacob nodded politely and put on his hat as he left the house. He climbed on his sleigh and headed to the post office.

"Well, hello there," a familiar voice spoke from inside the post office. Jacob looked over and there was Bert Hibbert.

"Hello, Bert," Jacob said. "How are you doing?"

"I'm getting along really well," Bert answered. "I found a few jobs here and there. I'm still staying at the Empire Hotel."

"That's great," Jacob said. "If I hear of anything, I will recommend you."

"That would be nice." Bert smiled. "It would be better to get a more permanent job."

"It was nice to see you, Bert," Jacob said as he went over to the postmaster.

"You have a letter yourself," the postmaster said with a big smile on his face.

"You don't say?" Jacob wasn't expecting anything in the mail. He held the letter and saw the familiar penmanship. His heart did a flip flop at the sight of her name in the top left-hand corner. It had been at least eight months since he had heard from Abigail, so he was quite taken aback. He had assumed that she thought it best if they didn't write anymore, since she would be married soon. Jacob had stopped writing to her. He put the letter in the pocket of his shirt to read when he got back home.

The ride home was a long one, or so it seemed to Jacob. He wanted desperately to see what was written in the letter, but at the same time he didn't. He felt that he should close that chapter of his life, since Abigail had moved on. But what if she came back? Maybe that was why she sent the letter? For a short moment, he forgot all about Anna. All he could think about was the beauty of his first love, how much he felt for Abigail. And then how it was never meant to be.

During supper Jacob wanted to talk to Mr. and Mrs. Rodgers about his visit with Mr. Adair. The letter was what he really had on his mind, though. He wanted to wait until he was at his house to read it, so he decided he would wait until after they had eaten.

"Well, it sounds like a fine idea," Mr. Rodgers exclaimed after Jacob told him about Mr. Adair's suggestion.

"Well, sir," Jacob said, "you have been like a father to me."

"Yes," Mr. Rodgers interrupted, "and a father would want to see his son blossom and do something amazing." He lit his cigar and sat back in his chair.

"Thank you, sir," Jacob said shyly. "You and Mrs. Rodgers have been so very kind to me."

"Jacob, my boy," Mr. Rodgers said seriously, "you have been good to us as well." Jacob smiled as he looked down at his finished plate.

"I just don't want to leave you without any help," Jacob said, with a worried face. "But, you know, I ran into Bert Hibbert today."

"Ah, Bert," Mr. Rodgers repeated. "How's the lad doing?"

"He's doing fine," Jacob said, "but he hasn't found permanent work yet."

"Oh?" Mr. Rodgers lifted his left eyebrow in surprise.

"I had an idea." Jacob was almost scared to ask the question. "If I leave to go to the village, how about Bert taking my place?"

"That's a fine idea, son," Mr. Rodgers exclaimed. "What a great idea." He clapped his hands together once.

"Well, sir," Jacob said, "I got the feeling that Bert is an honest, hard-working lad, and he really needs the steady income to bring his fiancé here as well."

"You're right, Jacob. I got that feeling as well."

"I guess it's settled then," Jacob said. "I will go back to town tomorrow and talk to Bert." He knew full well that Bert would take the job. "I will also speak with Mr. Adair. I can work here until the end of the month. That will give Bert time to get to know the place and I can show him the ropes before I leave."

"It's not like you will be very far away if I need you." Mr. Rodgers winked at him.

"Don't think we won't miss you," Mrs. Rodgers added. She was a little teary-eyed. She hugged Jacob and wiped her tears.

"Thank you for supper," Jacob said gratefully. There wouldn't be many more suppers together. He would definitely miss their visiting at the table each day, but he would be fulfilling his dream. Jacob quickly walked to his house, down the path he had walked for almost two years, to read Abigail's letter in private. He reached his door, went inside, and shut the door. He hung up his coat, took off his boots, lit a lamp and set it on the table. He then retrieved the letter from his pocket and ripped open the envelope, unfolded the letter, and began to read. It started with all the pleasantries of a usual letter. *"How are you? How is the weather? What have you been doing?"* And so on and so forth. Then he reached the reason for her letter:

> *...I just thought I would write one last time to tell you that Patrick and I have picked a date to be married. We will wed this fall, October the second. I wanted you to hear it from me. I will be finished school at the end of this spring so we thought it would be best to get married soon after. I wish you all the best and hope all your dreams will come true.*

> *With love,*
> *Abigail.*

Jacob's heart sank. In some fantasy, way in the back of his mind, he thought Abigail wouldn't get married and would come back to the prairies. But there went any possibility that Abigail would be his wife one day. Jacob sat down on the lounge in his living room and stared at the floor. Not that he didn't know this was supposed to happen. He just thought it wouldn't.

Jacob would have to carry on with his life. It seemed as if he had put it on hold for a while, trying to avoid the truth. His heart ached as if it were separated from his very being. He longed for the love he couldn't have. *Stop it!* he told himself. *Stop thinking of the old and start thinking about the new. There is a beautiful woman who wants you to love her.* He did love Anna, but there is a difference between your first love and every love afterward. Jacob felt like he wasn't being fair to Anna, but he knew he cared for her as she did for him.

chapter fourteen

The month went by fast. Today Jacob was moving to Abbington Pickets.

"Here, do you need this?" Bert asked as he held up a stool that looked like it belonged in the garbage.

"Yep," Jacob said, "I will take that with me." Bert had quickly learned the ropes at Goldenrod and he and Jacob had become good friends. Bert was helping Jacob move his belongings to the Empire Hotel. They filled the wagon with all Jacob's things. Although he didn't have much when he came to Goldenrod Ranch, Mr. Rodgers had given him a bed and a dresser to get him started and loaned him a few pieces of furniture until he could build his own. Mrs. Rodgers gave him bedding and kitchen items to help him start out.

Mr. and Mrs. Rodgers stood at the front door waiting to say their good-byes. Mrs. Rodgers was in her long grey dress and white apron with her black crocheted shawl wrapped around her shoulders. She had her arm looped in Mr. Rodgers'. Mr. Rodgers' pipe hung out of his mouth and puffs of smoke floated above his head.

The two men drove the wagon up to the front door, stopped, and climbed down. The wagon cover was still on the wagon from the fall. All the items in the back would be protected from falling or blowing out. Jacob's horse was tied to the wagon, as well.

"Oh, Jacob," Mrs. Rodgers cried. "We are going to miss you and your smiling face." She gave him a big hug.

"Good luck, Jacob." Mr. Rodgers shook his hand and then gave him a hug. "If there is anything you need, son, we are not far away."

"Thank you, sir," Jacob said sadly. "I will see you more often than you think," he added with a slight smile.

"I will get him settled, Mr. Rodgers," Bert reassured them, "and I will be back with the wagon."

"Thank you, Bert." Mr. Rodgers patted him on the back. "Glad you're here, lad."

Jacob and Bert climbed up on the wagon. Jacob held the reins and started the horses out the lane. He looked at Mr. and Mrs. Rodgers, tipped his hat, and nodded as they drove away. Jacob was sad to leave Goldenrod. The Rodgers were like parents to him. But all children need to leave the nest and go out on their own.

It was after dinner when they reached Abbington Pickets. The village was abuzz with people walking to and from buildings. Wagons met one another as they went down the street to their destinations. Music poured out of the Empire Hotel doors every time they were opened. Jacob drove the wagon to the back of the hotel, his residence for the time being. He opened the door and they started to unload the wagon and carry the heavy belongings into his new abode.

Mr. Adair had seen them driving by The General Store and came over to see them. "Jacob," he exclaimed. "This is a happy day!" He smiled from ear to ear.

"Yes, sir," Jacob replied with a smile as he put down the crate he was carrying.

"You won't regret this, my boy," Mr. Adair assured him.

"I hope not," Jacob said with a laugh. "I don't have a job at the Rodgers' anymore." He joked, but inside he was scared to death. *Was he making the right choice? Well, now is the time to find out.*

"Let me know if you need anything," Mr. Adair said. "I will let you get settled." He walked back across the street to his store.

It didn't take them long to carry the furniture into the one-room apartment. They set everything in the middle of the room. "I will arrange the furniture later," Jacob said, "and then I will unpack the crates."

"I'll help you put your bed together," Bert said. "It won't take us long."

"Knock, knock," said a woman's voice outside the door.

Jacob turned around and saw Anna. She was wearing a light blue dress with a white apron, and a pink wrap around her arms. Her beautiful blonde hair was in a neat braid to the side of her head and down one shoulder.

"Come in," he said with delight. "What a surprise this is indeed." He stood up from working on the bed frame and greeted her. "You remember Bert," Jacob asked, "don't you?"

"Yes, of course." Bert walked over and shook her hand.

"A pleasure, Miss Anna," Bert said. "It's good to see you again."

"I brought you some lunch." Anna held up her wicker picnic basket covered with a white and red checked cloth. "I knew you would be hungry," she said with a big smile. "I made your favourite." She had a twinkle in her eye when she looked at Jacob.

"You are an absolute doll," exclaimed Jacob. "I am starved." He picked Anna up, with his arms around her waist, and twirled her around the bare room. Anna giggled as Jacob went in circles.

"Okay, okay, okay," she squealed, "you're making me dizzy." Jacob stopped and put her down. "Now, how am I supposed to set the table, dizzy like this?" Anna could barely stand up straight.

"Oh, I will help you," Jacob offered as he grabbed a blanket from one of his crates and laid it out on the floor for a real picnic. Anna took her basket and set it on the blanket. Bert and Jacob sat down on the blanket with her. She set the "table" in the middle of the blanket, using the red and white check cloth as a tablecloth. She took out freshly-made egg salad sandwiches on homemade bread and dill pickles. She handed each of the men hot tea in mason jars. For dessert, Anna brought gingersnap cookies and white coconut cake.

"Mmmm," Jacob said, biting into his sandwich. "You sure know how to spoil a guy." He winked at Anna. Her cheeks went rosy and she shyly smiled back.

"Yes. You are so right," Bert agreed while devouring his own sandwich. "You are a great cook, Miss Anna," he complimented her.

"Thank you, Bert," she said to him. "I love to bake and cook."

It wasn't long until the picnic lunch was devoured and everyone had to get back to work.

"Well, I better get home," Anna announced. "I have a roast in the oven and I have to start getting ready for supper."

"Thank you, my dear girl," Jacob smiled. "That hit the spot." He rubbed his stomach.

"Yes," Bert added, "thank you." Jacob helped Anna gather her picnic basket and walked her outside the door. Bert proceeded to put the bed together.

"I meant it," Jacob started, "that was wonderful and very kind of you." He put his hands on her shoulders and pulled her closer to him, whispering, "thank you." He slowly brought his head down to hers, closed his eyes, and kissed her soft lips. He could taste the sweet flavour of the coconut cake she had eaten. Anna pulled away shyly, put her hand over her lips, and put her head down. Jacob could tell she was blushing.

"I am so sorry," Jacob said quickly as he stepped back away from her. "I didn't mean to...I mean, I didn't want to...I mean, I shouldn't have."

"It's okay," Anna said quietly. "I mean, I was just surprised." She smiled at him and then she looked down at her feet.

"I shouldn't have," Jacob said again as he stood with his arm up against the building.

"Really, it's alright," Anna said. "I better get going, though." She turned around and walked toward the street.

"Thanks again, Anna," Jacob called after her.

Anna turned around and waved, with a smile.

Darn, darn, darn! Why did I have to do that? He asked himself over and over. He was so angry with himself. He worried that he had upset Anna and would ruin any chance he had with her. *I am so stupid,* he told himself. He went back into the house to continue putting his belongings away and help Bert with the bed. All he could think about was Anna. He was disgusted with himself for kissing her without warning. Bert stayed for most of the afternoon and then left to go get his chores done.

Jacob sat down on his bed thinking about his life. He felt very alone. He didn't feel comfortable in his new abode. He had saved enough money to live for a couple of months without any income, but he was anxious to get started. Jacob lay back on his bed with his hands behind his head on the pillow. He thought about what he was going to do in the morning. He needed to organize his new store, and partition off the workshop and the living quarters. With all this weighing on his mind, he topped it off by thinking about Anna. *What was he going to say to her? And when?* He knew that he needed to go see her soon. Jacob closed his eyes and thought of Anna's beautiful face. Slowly he drifted off to sleep.

Jacob woke with the sun shining brightly in his eyes. *I guess it's time to find a curtain or some blinds for that window,* he told himself. He lay stretching his arms above his head and yawned. He was still in his clothes from yesterday, as he had fallen asleep before getting ready for bed. He realized, or at least his stomach realized, that he needed to do some shopping at The General Store. He got up and found a basin to wash up in. The face cloth and towel were still packed, but they were easy for him to locate. Ah! There was no water. Suddenly there was a knock at the door.

"Come in," Jacob hollered as he went to the door and opened it. What a sight for sore eyes. There stood Anna, with a pitcher of water and a basket of food.

"Good morning, sunshine!" Anna exclaimed.

"Well, good morning," Jacob said, with a surprised look on his face.

"I knew you wouldn't be set up too well yet," Anna explained. "Once father left for work, I decided to bring you some breakfast."

"Aren't you just an angel?" Jacob said, smiling. Realizing they were still standing at the door, he said, "Come in, come in." He backed away from the door to let Anna through the doorway.

"I see you have your bed and table set up," Anna observed.

"Yep," Jacob said proudly. "We don't have to sit on the floor this time." He laughed as he looked at the table and two chairs he had borrowed from Mr. Adair. Anna set the basket down on the table and started to unpack it. Jacob took the water jug and went to the other side of the room to discreetly wash up.

"Breakfast is served," Anna announced, just as Jacob finished combing his hair.

"Looks delicious." Jacob observed the biscuits, jam, butter, and hard-boiled eggs. Jacob helped Anna into her chair and they sat down at the table. Jacob said grace and they began to eat their breakfast. Jacob was grateful that he had Anna in his life; she had been a godsend. He tried to find the right words, at the right time, to bring up the kiss from yesterday. He felt so awkward about it that he thought of not mentioning it. It seemed as though it didn't bother Anna, or she wouldn't be here. On the other hand, he wanted to clear the air with her before they went any further.

He had started to care for Anna, more that he thought he could. She was such a kind-hearted woman, putting other people first without any thought for herself. Kind people like that just don't come along every day. Still, he felt guilty, suspecting that he might be using Anna as a replacement for Abigail. He pushed that thought out of his head. He had to move forward, he told himself. Abigail had a new life and he must carry on with his. Also, because Abigail didn't even know how Jacob felt, he couldn't really blame her, either.

"Anna." Jacob lifted his head and looked into Anna's eyes.

"Yes, Jacob," Anna replied as she looked at him.

"I hope I didn't ruin our friendship yesterday." He blurted it out and held his breath waiting for her response.

"Don't even give it another thought." Anna smiled as she looked at Jacob with her blue eyes. "Besides, I liked it," Anna stated matter-of-factly.

Shocked by her latter comment, Jacob was speechless. He sat with his mouth open for a few seconds.

"Is there anything I could help you with today?" she asked him. Jacob thought of all the housekeeping chores he had left to do, and that he needed to build partitions and get his shop set up.

"There are many things that need to be done, but you don't have to help. You have done enough already," he assured her.

"I want to help," Anna insisted. "You do what you need to and I'll start by doing the dishes."

"If you insist," Jacob gave in. "I need to go get a few supplies from The General Store. I won't be gone long."

"Alright," Anna said as she started picking up the plates. "I will be here. By the way, did anyone show you where to get your water?"

"No," Jacob answered with a confused look on his face.

"Well, there is a water pump across the street in front of the flour mill," Anna explained. "Some of us get our water from there. The rest have their own wells built into their homes."

"That explains it." Jacob was relieved to find out he didn't have to go very far for water. He went to see Mr. Adair to buy some lumber to build the partitions. He wasn't gone long, and when he came back he saw that Anna had already made a difference in his house.

"Wow. The place looks great," Jacob exclaimed. He saw that the crates were emptied and all his stuff put away. The stove was over to one side of the room, close to the wall, so Anna had started to make a kitchen there. She had moved the table over there as well, and even put a tablecloth on it, though Jacob didn't know where she had found it. Anna had used the wooden crates to set up a makeshift cupboard in the corner, and she had put the bowls, plates, and cups into it. She had moved his bed against the side wall and put a little side table next to it for him to wash up. The basin was placed on top, with a towel folded beside it.

Jacob was amazed at what she had done in such a short time.

"I like to make a house homey," Anna beamed. "It's my favourite thing to do."

"Well, you did an amazing job," Jacob complimented her design. "I got everything I need to start building."

"While you are doing that," Anna started to say, "I am going to go find you some groceries." She took her apron off and dusted the front of her dress.

"You really don't have to do that," Jacob repeated. "I can take care of it, really."

"I just want to help," Anna insisted. "Besides, I have all my chores done at home and have nothing else to do." She smiled sheepishly.

Jacob knew that wasn't really true. There were always chores to do, no matter who you were. "Alright," Jacob gave in, "just put it on my account."

"Sounds good," Anna said as she walked out the doorway. "I will be back." She turned her head and was gone.

Jacob began to build the frame for the partition to divide the living quarters and the workshop. He worked in the middle of the floor. He would construct it lying down and then lift it up into place when it was complete.

The day went by fast. Jacob built the partition and Anna helped him stand it up and attach it to the wall and floor. They stood back and admired their work. Anna had bought enough food to last Jacob a week. They had accomplished quite a lot. "Come have supper with us," Anna told Jacob. "We are having leftover roast from last night; it won't take me long to have it ready."

"What would your father say?" Jacob asked.

"He would love the company," she answered.

"Well..." Jacob hesitated.

"It's settled then," she said. She gathered her things and they walked to Anna's house for supper.

chapter fifteen

It had been a couple months since Jacob had moved to Abbington Pickets and made the back room of the Empire Hotel his home and workplace. Anna helped him almost every day. She became quite the little carpenter. They finished building the two walls and created the front of the store to show off his masterpieces. Anna helped make his house a home, even sewed curtains for the windows. Mr. Adair returned all the tables he had left in stock from the winter, so Jacob would have furniture to sell right away. Business wasn't exactly booming, but it was a great start. He sold his first table the first week he was open for business, and had several special orders for side tables from local ladies.

Jacob's relationship with Anna blossomed. Anna's father had also taken a shine to Jacob, and he had supper there at least three or four times a week. Sunday church services were a regular outing for the two of them. Jacob saw his brothers more often, since they would stop in to see him when they came to town for supplies. He had seen his mother twice without his father, and had been able to have a nice visit.

He and Anna also managed to attend the Abbington Pickets horse races. It was one of the village's forms of entertainment.

People came from far and wide to watch and bet on the local horses. One horse in particular was a winner, and wealthy Americans came from the United States to bet on him. His name was Trooper. Originally, he had belonged to the Benedict brothers, but he had been sold when they moved away. He now belonged to the Howards and was still the talk of the village.

"The sign looks great," exclaimed Mr. Adair. He walked up behind Jacob, who was admiring his creation. Mr. Adair had a rolled-up newspaper under his arm.

"Thank you," Jacob said with a grin. He couldn't help but be proud of his new sign, now mounted above the door of his storefront. "I just finished it last night and couldn't wait to nail it up first thing this morning." The two men stood looking at the white words painted on the black background: "Hudson's Carpentry Est. 1908." The sign was constructed of wood and measured two feet by four feet.

Mr. Adair patted Jacob on the back, showing his approval.

"You'll do great, son," he said to Jacob.

"I sure hope so," Jacob replied. He thought of how his life had changed. Never did he think he would be in business for himself, not to mention be in love with a wonderful woman. Life was amazing. He felt a sensation of warmth, excitement, and great satisfaction.

"Oh, by the way," Mr. Adair handed Jacob the newspaper, "thought you might like to read the news. King Edward VII has died, and we now have King George V. God save the King."

"Oh, my," Jacob exclaimed. "That's sad, but I'm sure he will be a great king, just as his father was."

"I am sure you're right, my lad," Mr. Adair agreed.

"Good morning, sunshine," sounded a familiar voice.

"Good morning to you too." Jacob turned to greet Anna with a smile and a kiss on the cheek.

"Wow. You finished it!" she exclaimed, admiring Jacob's work.

"Yep," Jacob said proudly as the three of them stood together.

"It looks amazing," Anna declared.

"Thank you." Jacob looked down at Anna, feeling her love through her words.

"Well, I will let you get back to work," announced Mr. Adair, with a wink at Jacob. "I know I have to." He walked across the street toward his store. Horses with wagons loped down the street and the noises of the village were in full swing.

"How about I make you some breakfast," Anna said to Jacob. "I know you haven't eaten yet."

"How do you know that?" Jacob asked. "I may have made the brunch of the year," he joked.

"Because, Mr. Hudson," she smiled with a twinkle in her eye and straightened the buttons on the collar of his shirt, "I know you so well," she said matter-of-factly.

They walked into Jacob's home holding hands and smiling. As Anna prepared fried eggs and toast, Jacob washed up and set the table. Soon they sat down to eat their morning meal. Jacob thought Anna made the best fried eggs. They were even better than Mrs. Rodgers'. He was just wiping his face with his napkin when a knock came at the door. The person didn't wait for an answer; the door burst open and in came Jacob's older brother, Peter.

"Jacob!" he shouted, in a panic, as he walked in. "It's Mama," he stated. "There's been a terrible accident."

"What are you saying?" Jacob didn't understand what his brother was trying to tell him. He stood up from his chair. He saw anguish on his brother's face and knew the news was not good. "Who was in an accident?" he demanded, as fear coursed through his body.

"Ma and Pa were coming back from Abbington Lake. There was a deer and then Mama fell." Peter was talking so fast that Jacob could hardly understand what he was trying to say.

"And what happened?" Jacob asked fiercely, anxiously waited to hear what he had to say. Peter was still trying to catch his breath as he continued to tell Jacob the story.

"A deer jumped out from the trees and spooked the horses. They took off and ran faster and faster. They must have run over a big rock, because Mama fell from the wagon."

"Oh, my gosh!" Jacob gasped.

"Pa tried to stop the horses," Peter continued. "When he finally did..." He turned away to gain his composure.

"Are they all right?" Jacob desperately searched his face for the answer he wanted to hear. His brother bowed his head, shaking it from side to side. Jacob's heart sank down to his stomach. He didn't want the reality of the truth. He wanted to be anywhere but there at that moment.

"Mama's gone," Peter said quietly. He was still shaking his head. There were tears in his eyes and he choked up when he said it.

"Noooooooooo!" Jacob said in desperation. "Are you sure?" he asked.

"Pa ran to her as fast as he could," Peter said. "Doc said her neck broke when she fell."

"No! It can't be true," Jacob pleaded with Peter, grabbing his arms with both hands. He didn't want to believe what his brother was telling him. Anna reached out to Jacob, held onto his arm, and gently pulled him back. He turned around and wrapped his arms around her and held her.

"I am so sorry, Jacob." Anna held him. Jacob clung to her like he never wanted to let go. All he felt was sorrow and loss. He knew that he would never see his mama again.

"I should have made more of an effort," Jacob started to say. "I should have tried harder. Stood up to Pa."

"Little brother," Peter consoled, "don't beat yourself up. You know how Pa is." He stood behind him, rubbing his back and trying to console him.

"If I would never have left," Jacob was still making excuses, "maybe this wouldn't have happened."

"Everything happens for a reason," Peter said plainly. "Only God knows the reason."

"Are you saying God wanted her to die?" Jacob demanded.

"Jacob, you know I am not saying that," Peter said sternly.

"I need to go see her, one more time," Jacob said.

"I don't think that is such a good idea, Jacob," Peter told him.

"Why? She is my mother too; I have a right to go see her," he said stubbornly.

"Maybe you better wait until tomorrow," Peter said.

"I don't want to wait. I want to go now." Jacob looked at Anna. "I have to go. I will be back."

"Jacob, maybe I should go with you," Anna suggested.

"I need to do this alone," he said and walked past Peter and out the doorway. He saddled his horse, mounted, and galloped away.

All the things he should have done ran through his mind. He should have stood up to his father when he had the chance. He should have told his mother about Lucy. It would have saved her so much worry. He should have told his father that he knew what happened. The more he thought, the angrier he became; he even felt anger toward God. *Why couldn't it have been his father dead instead of his precious mother? Why God, why?* He couldn't stop feeling anger toward his father, as if it was his father's fault that his mother was dead. *It was his fault!* That's what Jacob kept telling himself.

Jacob rode so fast that he saw the stone house before he knew it. It hadn't changed a bit since the night he had left. He climbed off his horse, tied her to the hitching post, and walked toward the house.

"Where do you think you're going?" The voice seemed to come out of nowhere. His father stood in the front doorway. Jacob hadn't seen him there when he rode up.

"I am here to see Ma," Jacob said frankly.

"Go back to your other family," his father yelled. "You don't belong here anymore."

"I am here to see Mama," Jacob said, "one last time."

"I said go away." Pa started to walk toward Jacob. "I don't want you here." His father didn't look well. His shirt was ripped and soiled. His britches had holes in both knees. He appeared confused and angry, and didn't seem to be his usual self.

For a moment, Jacob felt sorry for his father. He even felt remorse for wishing him dead and blaming him for his mother's death. It was quite obvious that he was hurting too. Despite his father telling him to leave, Jacob felt compelled to help him. His father stood before him and continued to tell him to leave.

"I am not leaving until I see my mother." Jacob stood firm.

"Jacob, Jacob, Jacob." Jane came running from the house. "I am so glad you are here," she exclaimed as she hugged him tightly. "Isn't it terrible?" Jane cried on Jacob's shoulder. "We haven't been so sad since little Lucy disappeared."

"I know. It's awful," Jacob consoled her. "I can't believe she is really gone."

"It's the worst day ever," she continued, unable to stop crying.

"Where are Andrew and Sarah?" Jacob asked.

"Sarah is at Kingston," she answered, "helping a friend get ready for a wedding. Andrew has gone to get her."

"I think you better leave," his father said again.

"Pa, leave Jacob alone," Jane said. "We need him right now. We need all the family we have."

"He isn't family anymore," Pa said with a sneer on his face, "or have you forgotten how he left us all a few years ago?" He paced back and forth in front of Jacob and Jane. "You are dead to me." He pointed his finger in Jacob's face.

"Stop it!" Jane yelled.

"I don't want to cause any trouble," Jacob said calmly. "Just let me see Mama, and I will leave."

"You can't anyway!" his father yelled.

"Pa! Please." Jane pushed her father gently back with her hand. She turned toward Jacob. "Jacob, Ma isn't here."

"Well, where is she?" Jacob questioned.

"She is at Doc's in Abbington Pickets," Jane answered. "He is bringing her home."

"Alright, I will go there," Jacob said. Just then a horse galloped up the lane toward them as they stood in the front yard. It was Peter.

"Whoa." Peter pulled on the reins and his horse came to a complete stop.

"Why didn't you tell me Mama wasn't even here?" Jacob said angrily.

"I tried. You wouldn't listen," Peter said. "You just ran off and left us standing there."

"I'm sorry." Jacob felt bad for leaving so abruptly.

Peter turned and quietly said to Jacob, "Anna is worried about you."

"With Pa's wagon ruined, Mr. MacDonald took Mama straight to Doc's," Jane explained. "He said he would bring her home so we could get her ready for the funeral." She was still very upset, but the tension between Jacob and their father seemed to make everyone forget why they were standing there.

A wagon and horses came into the yard. It was Doc and Reverend Young. They pulled the wagon close to the door to carry Mrs. Hudson inside. The sight of her in the back of the wagon, knowing it was her under the blankets, made Jacob start to cry. He ran over to the wagon and climbed into the back.

"Son," Doc said softly, "wait until we get her inside." He tried to coax Jacob off the wagon. Mr. Hudson walked away and went into the house through the back doorway.

"Just let me see her!" Jacob exclaimed. He started to sob when he lifted the blanket to see his mother one last time.

Her skin was very pale and pasty. Jacob thought that she didn't look like herself, but she did look peaceful. He kissed her forehead and whispered to her so no one else could hear, "Now you and Lucy are together in heaven." Jacob wiped his eyes, stood up, jumped off the wagon, and ran toward his horse. He untied her and climbed on as quickly as he could, galloping down the lane without saying a word to anyone.

The next few days were a blur to Jacob. Anna was with him as much as she could be, helping him with anything he needed. Mostly he just needed someone to comfort him and be there for him.

Jacob wanted to build his mother's casket. His father argued about it, but gave in. So, with a tear-stained face and much love in his heart, he built his mother's final resting place. It was the hardest thing he had ever had to do.

The day of the funeral was a terrible time for the whole family. His father didn't want Jacob attending the funeral, but his siblings argued that Jacob should be there. It was uncomfortable for Jacob. He felt like the black sheep of the family but he wanted to be there for his Mama. The service was a celebration of her life. The whole village and surrounding community attended. Mrs. Hudson had been a well-liked woman in the community. Reverend Young spoke highly of her cooking and her contributions to the church and the women's prayer group. After the service she was buried in the church graveyard.

Jacob and Anna stood over his mother's grave with tulips in their hands. They were her favourite flowers. As Jacob knelt down, a tear rolled down his cheek. He quickly wiped it away with the back of his hand. He placed the flowers on her grave and knelt there for a few minutes. Anna stood beside him. Jacob was wearing his best suit, but he didn't care if he got it dirty kneeling in the dirt.

Everyone who attended the funeral said their condolences to each family member individually, as they left the graveside.

"I am so very sorry, Jacob," Mr. and Mrs. Adair said sympathetically. Mr. Adair shook his hand with deep concern. Once the last person had ridden away, Jacob felt very alone. His family was still there, but he wasn't close to any of them anymore. The only one who had made him feel like he belonged was Ma; now that she was gone, he didn't feel like he had a place anymore.

Jacob hugged his sisters and then his brothers before they left for home. His father was already sitting in the wagon waiting for the girls to get in. It was obvious that his father was going to hold this grudge forever. Now that Mama was gone, it would be even harder for him to go back home again.

Jacob and Anna walked hand in hand to Jacob's home. Jacob was in a daze and wanted to sleep. He wished he could wake up and this nightmare would be over.

chapter sixteen

The early morning sun shone brightly through the window of Jacob's workshop. His nightmares about Lucy had begun again. Jacob worked diligently, sanding a side table to prepare it for the final finish. It had been two and a half months since the funeral. Jacob tried to keep himself extremely busy, every hour of every day, to keep his mind off his mother's death. One day turned into another as he went through the motions of everyday life. When Jacob wasn't working in the workshop he was with Anna on an outing of some sort, either a picnic in the trees or a fox hunt with the club from Abbington Pickets.

"Jacob." Anna came in from outside with a bouquet of wildflowers in her hand. "I thought these would brighten up the room." She showed Jacob her arrangement proudly.

"They are beautiful," Jacob said with a weak smile, "just like the angel that brought them." He gave Anna a wink. She went over to the cupboard and got a jar to put the flowers in.

"I have water in the jug by the window. You can use that for the flowers," Jacob suggested. Anna arranged the flowers and placed them in the middle of the kitchen table.

"Looks amazing," Jacob observed as he walked up behind Anna and put his arms around her. She leaned her head back on his chest and held his arms in front of her with her hands. They stood there in quiet bliss, enjoying the moment. The top of Anna's head reached Jacob's lips. The fragrance of her hair delighted his inner body.

"I wish," Jacob whispered, "I could make time stand still like this." He held her tighter. Anna turned around and Jacob embraced her with his strong arms as she nestled her head in his chest.

"So do I," Anna said softly.

Their quiet moment in time was abruptly interrupted. *Knock, knock, knock,* came at the door.

"Hello, Jacob," a voice said, "it's me, Mr. Adair."

Jacob quickly let go of Anna and walked toward the door. He grabbed the latch with his right hand and opened it.

"Good morning, sir," Jacob said. He felt a little sheepish, since it was so early in the morning and Anna was standing in the room. He didn't want Mr. Adair to assume there was something going on that wasn't proper.

"Good morning, Jacob," Mr. Adair said. "It's a beautiful day, isn't it?"

"Sure is." Jacob smiled and looked back at Anna with a wink, which, of course, Mr. Adair couldn't see. He turned his head back and asked, "What can I do for you, sir?"

"Well, Jacob," Mr. Adair began as he took off his hat and held it in his hands in front of him. He seemed slightly distracted. "I have a proposition for you."

"Really?" Jacob was curious.

"I received an order for some fur from Kingston," Mr. Adair continued. "They also requested six of your tables, if you have them."

"Oh, sure, I have several in stock." Jacob was excited to hear of the order. "Over here." He stepped back to show him the tables lined up along the wall.

"Ah, that's mighty fine," Mr. Adair complimented him as he touched the top of one table, feeling its smoothness. "Excellent work, my boy," he declared with a satisfied smile.

"Thank you, sir," Jacob said, pleased with the compliment. His chest seemed to puff up with pride.

"Would you be able to go to Kingston to deliver the tables?" Mr. Adair asked. "When do you want me to go?" Jacob smiled at the offer.

"As soon as you can arrange it," Mr. Adair replied. "I realize it's quite a drive." He looked at Anna. "Maybe you could take someone with you?" He smiled.

Jacob blushed, and so did the fair-complexioned young lady. "What do you say?" Jacob looked at Anna. "Would you like to come?" he asked.

"I would love to." Anna smiled. "But I'll check with Pa first."

"Alright then," Mr. Adair said, "you get it all figured out, Jacob. You can take my wagon and team." He put his hat back on and left.

"What will people say?" Anna questioned. "It isn't very ladylike to be alone with a man, you know."

"Don't worry, Anna," Jacob reassured her. "We know that we are doing nothing wrong, so don't worry so much about what other people think."

"I know, Jacob," she said, with a concerned look on her face, "but Pa may not let me go without a chaperone."

"We haven't the time to find one, little lady," Jacob told her. "You heard what Mr. Adair said. We have to go right away." He touched the tip of her nose with his finger just to tease her.

"Stop that," she giggled.

"Stop what?" he teased. "I didn't do anything."

"You know what I mean!" she exclaimed.

"No, I don't," he continued. "What do you mean?" He laughed at the stern look on her face.

"You do so." She tried not to laugh. "You're such a tease, Jacob Hudson!" Jacob started to tickle Anna in the side of the ribs. She giggled and twisted and turned to make him stop, but he was stronger than her. Anna crouched down on the floor on her knees and then fell right down on the floor as Jacob continued to tickle her.

"Alright! Alright! I give up!" she yelled as he hovered over her on the floor. She huffed and puffed, exhausted from laughing. Jacob stopped and sat on the floor beside her. He admired her beautiful smile and thought that no matter what she was doing, she looked amazing. Jacob held his hand out to help her stand up.

"You are so much fun to tease," Jacob joked.

"And you are such a pain." Anna tried to pretend that she was angry but it was apparent that she wasn't. They both burst out laughing.

"You always make me feel good," Jacob told Anna. "I am so grateful for waking up on your porch that day." He swiped the hair from her forehead and put it back into place.

"Me too." She smiled. "I better go talk to Pa and finish up my chores."

"Yes, I need to finish these tables." Anna left and Jacob continued his carpentry.

The next day Jacob loaded the covered wagon with his furniture and Mr. Adair's goods. He tied each piece so that there would be no shifting. The tables were wrapped in cotton sheets so they wouldn't get scratched. Jacob packed his bag with food, water, and bedding. He hitched up the horses and put a closed sign, stating that he would be back in a week, on his door. He drove up to The General Store to say his farewell to Mr. Adair and then headed over to Anna's.

Anna stood on her porch with her luggage and her good old picnic basket beside her. She wore her pink dress with white lace trim. She had on her white shawl and carried her parasol. Jacob hopped off the wagon and walked toward the house. The front door opened and Anna's father appeared.

"Good morning, Jacob," he was greeted with a handshake. "I just wanted to talk to you before the two of you left."

"Alright, sir," Jacob replied.

"Come into the house and sit for a minute." Anna's father held the door open. He was wearing his leather apron; it was apparent he had come from work and was soon going back. Jacob took off his hat and held it in his hand as he walked in.

"Here, sit," he directed Jacob and then sat down as well.

"You have separate bedding for the trip?" he questioned.

"You bet," Jacob said.

"Once you get to Kingston," he continued, "you will be sleeping in separate accommodations?"

"Of course, sir," Jacob said.

"Letting you two go without a chaperone," her father said seriously, "is not very proper."

Jacob looked straight at Anna's father. "Sir, I give you my word that I will treat Anna with the utmost respect," he said assuredly.

"I know you will, son," her father said. "I just needed to hear you say it." He stood up and patted Jacob on the back of the shoulder. Jacob got up, gave Anna's father a reassuring smile, and they walked back outside. "Have a safe trip," he added, "and see you in a week."

"Thank you, sir." Jacob nodded.

Anna's father walked back over to where Anna was standing and hugged her. "Good-bye Pa," she said as she hugged him back. "I will be back before you know it. Make sure you don't skip meals just because I'm not here," she scolded her father as he helped her onto the wagon.

"I won't." He smiled at her. "But I am not a very good cook, as you well know."

"There is leftover venison in the ice box," she instructed, "and enough homemade bread to last you a week."

"You look like you're ready to go," Jacob interrupted their conversation, wanting to get on the road to Kingston.

Anna continued to tell her father how to cook and do without her. Jacob climbed on and grabbed the reins. They both waved to Anna's father. "Hee-ya," Jacob said to the horses and they started to trot. They were on their way. It was the first time Jacob had travelled this far from home. It seemed like an adventure.

The scenery along the way was magnificent. It was late summer and there were wildflowers blooming: purple asters, black-eyed Susans, and goldenrod. The grass grew high and blew in the wind like a flowing river. The trees were starting to turn yellow and made for a pretty palette. Every mile they travelled they saw something new. They saw a cow moose and her baby in the distance, and deer travelling in a herd.

"Look over there!" Anna said with delight. "No, over there." She pointed to a little brown jackrabbit running into the trees to hide. Jacob smiled with amusement over Anna's pleasure at nature's pasture.

"Isn't he cute," she declared.

"Oh, very cute." Jacob smiled and kept his hands on the reins. They had travelled a good part of the day. They were almost halfway to Kingston and would be staying at the stopping house tonight.

"There is a beautiful spot over there." Anna pointed toward a lonely tree in the middle of a grass plain close to what looked like a slough. "Why don't we stop there for a bite to eat?"

"Good idea," Jacob agreed. "The horses need a rest and water." Jacob turned the horses in the direction Anna was pointing. "Whoa." Jacob pulled the reins to stop the horses near the water. He unhitched them and held their reins while he walked them over for a drink. Anna prepared their little picnic lunch. She spread a blanket on the grass under the tree, where it was shady. She climbed back into the wagon to retrieve her basket of food and laid everything out on the blanket. When Jacob had finished with the horses, he tied them to a tree to graze. He walked over and sat down on the corner of the pastel-coloured blanket and pulled off his boots.

"Wow." Jacob smiled. "This looks good. I sure am hungry."

"Of course you are," Anna giggled. "You're a man." They ate the venison sandwiches Anna had made, along with a jar of cold tea and Anna's famous ginger cookies. They couldn't rest long, as they still had a long trip ahead of them and they didn't want to travel much in the dark.

Jacob hitched the horses to the wagon again and Anna packed what remained of their picnic lunch. They climbed back up on the wagon seat and soon were back on the trail. The trip seemed longer as it got closer to nightfall. Jacob's back was sore from the long hours of bouncing on the seat. He couldn't imagine how Anna felt, even though she never complained one bit. He surely could see why the people of Abbington Pickets never left the village much.

Jacob and Anna had driven for a few hours into the night and could finally see the light of the stopping house, where travellers could stay on the long stretch to Kingston. It was a square, white-washed building with windows, one door, and a little lighthouse on top. There was a stable next to the house with hay and oats for travellers to use if they didn't bring any of their own.

"There it is," Jacob said tiredly. "We can sleep for a while now," he reassured Anna with a tired smile.

"I've been sleeping already," Anna exclaimed, even though she wasn't nearly as tired as Jacob. She had nodded off a few times while they were on the road. They reached the stopping house. Jacob helped Anna down from the wagon and pulled out their bags and bedding.

"I will go water and feed the horses while you get set up inside," he told Anna as he unhitched the horses in a daze.

"Okay," she yawned. "See you inside." It was apparent that no one else was traveling on this night, because the stopping house was empty. Inside the house was a stove, with a kitchen area on one side and cots set up on the other. The cots were empty, as people brought their own bedding. Anna made their beds with the sheets and blankets they had brought with them.

Jacob opened the door and came in. "The horses are bedded down for the night," he said. "I don't think I could even eat, I'm so tired."

"I set some biscuits and water out for you," Anna said. "We haven't eaten much. You should eat a little," she coaxed.

Jacob sat on the edge of the cot with a biscuit in his hand. He had a bite or two and a drink of water and then leaned down onto his bed and dozed off. Anna crawled into the cot next to him and fell asleep as well.

A few hours later, in the middle of the night, there was a loud bang and the door slammed shut. Jacob sat straight up in his bed. His heart began to pound with fear. He looked over and saw Anna lying very still, with her eyes open and looking straight at him. Jacob put his finger over his lips.

"Who's there?" he demanded.

"It's no one but me." A slurred voice came from the doorway.

"Who are you?" Jacob asked.

"My name," the voice stammered, "...is...Jim." He continued to slur his words and seemed to stumble as he walked. He was surely drunk, and Jacob knew it. "Don't worry about me," Jim said. "I will just sleep over here." He stumbled to a cot close to Anna.

"Maybe you should sleep in this one over here." Jacob pointed to the one on the other side of him. He wanted to keep an eye on Jim. Jacob didn't feel safe with a drunk stranger anywhere near Anna. He looked back over at Anna, to make sure she was all right. She looked frozen in one spot.

"I am good here," the stranger said. He seemed to be a little agitated.

"I'm scared," Anna whispered to Jacob. He could see fear in her eyes.

"It's all right," Jacob soothed, "I think he's harmless." He was trying not to let on that he was just as worried. Then Jacob heard movement. The man got up and stumbled around again. He walked about, banging into the cots, until he reached Anna's cot. With a terrifying look on his face, with only the light of the moon coming in the window, he could see she was there.

"Who's in my bed?" The stranger seemed to get angry. "Hey. Get out of my bed," he demanded. He patted the blankets.

"Jim." Jacob raised his voice a little and tried to sound stern. "That's my wife's bed. Yours is over there." He pointed in the other direction. Jacob could hear Anna breathing fearfully. He thought that if he told the stranger she was his wife, he would be less likely to bother her.

"Oh, sorry, Mrs." the stranger slurred, stumbling back to his original cot. Jacob and Anna lay as still as possible and soon they heard the stranger snoring.

"Jacob," Anna whispered, "I'm so scared. Let's leave."

"We should sleep a little longer," Jacob whispered back. "He's harmless. He just has to sleep it off," he tried to reassure her. He knew they needed a few more hours of sleep. "We will get up and sneak out of here before he wakes up."

"Are you sure?" Anna pleaded. "I'm worried."

"Here." Jacob lifted his blanket up. "Crawl in with me. He won't bother you, I promise."

Anna slowly climbed out of her bed. She stood hunched over so as not to make any movement that the stranger might see. She crawled in beside Jacob, and he placed the covers back over the two of them. Both Anna and Jacob still wore their clothes. As inappropriate as this would appear to anyone walking in the doorway, Jacob knew nothing would happen. Even though he was more than happy to share the space with Anna, and be as close to her as he possibly could be, it was a tight fit. The cot was only meant for one person, but neither of them minded the tight quarters. Jacob had one arm under Anna's neck and his other arm over her to keep her from falling off the cot. They dozed off to sleep.

A few hours later, when the sun was just about to come up, Jacob awoke. He looked over at Anna's peaceful face. She was still sound asleep. His heart went flip flop, just as it used to with Abigail. As much as he would have loved to stay in that position all morning, admiring her beautiful face, he knew they needed to get up and out of there before the stranger in the other cot woke up. Jacob leaned up and kissed Anna's forehead.

"Wake up, sleepy head," he whispered. Anna's eyes slowly opened and she immediately smiled. She didn't say a word, but she looked over to see if the stranger was still there and saw that he was. They climbed out of the bed, gathered their bedding and food, and tiptoed outside. Anna placed their belongings into the wagon while Jacob went to get the horses and hitch up the wagon. Jacob saw the stranger's horses still hitched to his wagon. He shook his head. *Poor horses*, he thought. *I guess he'll be getting up soon.* He brought the horses some water and oats to tide them over until their owner woke up. Before long they were back on their way to Kingston.

"I sure hope the rest of the trip is less eventful," Jacob stated. "That guy almost gave me a heart attack."

"Me too," agreed Anna, with a relieved look on her face. "I must look a mess, leaving in such a hurry and sleeping in my clothes, no less." She looked down at her wrinkled dress and tried to smooth it out with her hands.

"Well," Jacob smiled, "you're not the only one. I didn't get a chance to beautify myself this morning either," he teased.

"Oh, you," Anna declared. "You know what I mean." She play-slapped him on the arm. Anna reached for the food behind their seat and gave Jacob a sandwich. They decided to eat on the way, since they hadn't taken time to have breakfast before they left.

Jacob and Anna reached Kingston that evening, just before dark. Kingston was a lot bigger than Abbington Pickets. Jacob was in awe of how many houses were in town. They drove down what looked to be the main street. Mr. Adair had told Jacob that he and Anna could stay with his brother and sister-in-law; they lived in a blue house a little way off Main Street. As they drove down the street, they saw the hotel. There was loud music and yelling coming from the saloon. Jacob stopped in front of the hotel to have a look around. Lingering outside the saloon door were girls dressed in clothes unlike any Jacob had ever seen before. They wore bright red dresses with their cleavages showing. Their faces were painted with makeup. Jacob continued on, surprised that people presented themselves that way.

The horses trotted until they reached the only blue house on the street. It had been easy to find the right house, after all. Jacob drove the horses to the front of Mr. Adair's brother's house. Both Jacob and Anna stood up and stretched before they got off the wagon. At that moment, a couple appeared from the house. They walked up their walkway and out to the gate enclosing their yard.

"You must be Jacob," exclaimed the nice-looking gentleman, as he stood with his arm around his wife.

"Yes, sir," Jacob admitted. "I sure am, and this is Anna." He pointed to his beautiful Anna.

"Wonderful," the man said. "I am Mr. David Adair, and this is my wife, Lily, Mrs. Adair," he introduced. "Just call us David and Lily." He smiled and held Anna's hand as she jumped off the wagon.

"I'm sure you folks are tired after that long drive," Mrs. Adair said. "Come in, Anna, while the men put away the horses." She put her arm around Anna and led her into the house. Mrs. Adair was a sweet-looking lady with wavy blonde hair up in a bun. Her green eyes sparkled with kindness. She had a black shawl around her shoulders and wore a grey dress. Mr. Adair looked a lot like his brother and reminded Jacob of him. It was weird to call two different men "Mr. Adair," Jacob thought to himself.

Jacob and David unhitched the horses, fed them, and gave them water. "We will unload the wagon in the morning," David said as they left the wagon and went into the blue two-storey house. It had white trim and a highly-crafted wraparound porch.

Inside, the house was beautifully decorated, and Jacob noticed one of his tables perfectly perched between two chairs in the drawing room. "This looks familiar." Jacob smiled as he touched the top of the piece.

"I bet it does." Lily was delighted that he had noticed. "I have friends who want tables built by you." She smiled. Jacob realized why he had brought six tables to Kingston.

"We will talk about that in the morning, over breakfast," announced David.

Lily showed Jacob and Anna to their rooms. Jacob admired the craftsmanship throughout the house. The upstairs banisters were beautifully hand-carved. It was obvious that Lily was a wonderful decorator. He observed the floral wallpaper and the matching drapes. Jacob's room was quaint, with a handmade blue and white quilt on the bed. The quilt matched the white trim and blue walls. *So, this is how town people live,* Jacob thought to himself.

Morning came quickly and everyone gathered around the breakfast table. It was draped with a lace tablecloth and held matching dishes and cutlery. Jacob noticed how lovely Anna looked this morning. Today she wore her blue dress with white lace trimming the sleeves and neckline.

"Did you sleep well?" Lily asked Jacob.

"Yes, thank you, ma'am." Jacob nodded.

"I was thinking," Lily began, "why don't you and Anna stay one more day?" She looked at Jacob, then at Anna.

"Well," Jacob started as he quickly glanced at Anna to see how she had reacted, "I'm not sure."

"Sure. We don't mind," Anna interrupted with a smile. "Do we, Jacob?" She grinned from ear to ear with a twinkle in her eye.

"It's settled then," Lily stated. "I will prepare a wonderful supper." Lily was excited, like a child getting a Christmas present.

"Well, now that that's settled," David said, "Jacob, I hope you have more of those tables at home." He smiled as he held his fork in his hand.

"I sure do, sir," Jacob answered, "and I have even more that are partially made."

"Good, good," David said, taking a big bite of his eggs on toast.

"All my friends love your work," Lily remarked.

"Thank you." Jacob smiled.

"I was thinking," David said, "if I could get a driver to go back and forth from Abbington Pickets to Kingston once a month, could you have at least six or maybe eight tables made for the trip?"

"Wow, sir." Jacob stopped chewing. He swallowed and wiped his mouth with a napkin. He was surprised by the proposition. "That's quite a few tables, but I am sure I could do six."

"Well, I believe I can sell them at my store," David said. He had a general store in Kingston, just like his brother's. "The ladies around here seem to love them. They keep asking us where we got ours."

"Thank you, sir," Jacob said gratefully, "for this wonderful opportunity." Jacob realized how this could affect his business. If he could sell that many tables here and some at home, he could make quite a profit. He could afford to build his own house and propose to Anna. Jacob had many things going through his mind at that moment.

Breakfast was finished. Jacob and David went outside to unload the tables and the goods Mr. Adair had sent to his brother. David paid Jacob for the tables he had delivered.

Jacob spent most of the day with David. They loaded the wagon with the stock he wanted to send back to his brother. Anna spent her time with Lily, baking and preparing supper. Lily informed them that she had invited a few of their friends for supper, to meet Jacob, the famous "master table constructor," as she put it.

Neither Jacob nor Anna had packed fancy attire, so they wore what they had. Jacob felt like he didn't meet the clothing standards for the evening, but there wasn't anything he could do about it. "Don't you look stunning, my dear," Jacob said, in a pretend hoity-toity fashion.

"Why thank you, my lord." Anna giggled, not able to keep a straight face when Jacob bowed and kissed the back of her hand.

"You do look beautiful," Jacob said sincerely.

"And you look very handsome," Anna said sweetly.

"Shall we?" Jacob gave his arm to Anna. She put her arm in his and they walked down the stairs to meet everyone in the dining room.

"There he is," Lily exclaimed as they entered the room. Everyone looked toward Jacob and Anna. "This is our Jacob. The master table constructor," she told them with a big smile. She introduced Jacob to all her friends. "Jacob, this is Judy, she has bought two of your designs," Lily explained.

"How do you do, Jacob?" Judy said politely. "We all love your work, and look forward to seeing more."

"Thank you, ma'am," Jacob said as he shook her hand.

"This is my husband, Henry," she introduced them.

"And this is Rose and her husband Don," Lily stated. They shook hands with Jacob and Anna.

Lily had roast beef for supper, with mashed potatoes, gravy, and corn on the cob. The visiting around the table was entertaining, to say the least. The women had their fun flirting with Jacob, commending him on his wonderful talent, while the men admired Anna and made light conversation.

After supper, everyone proceeded into the drawing room for more visiting. David turned the handle on the gramophone to wind it up for some music. The quiet room filled with Scott Joplin's "Weeping Willow." Lily and David began dancing in the middle of the room and waved to encourage everyone else to join them.

"Could I have this dance, Miss Anna?" Jacob politely asked, holding out his hand for hers.

"Why certainly, my dear Mr. Hudson." She did a little curtsey in a joking way, taking Jacob's hand. Jacob put his arm around her waist and held her tightly. It was just like the dance at the Howards' last fall. Jacob wanted to hold Anna closer, but knew that he shouldn't.

"Would you like to take a walk?" he whispered in Anna's ear. "It's a beautiful night." Anna smiled and nodded in agreement.

When the song ended, Jacob and Anna stepped aside as David changed the song on the gramophone. "It's such a wonderful night," Jacob announced. "Anna and I are going for a walk."

"Good idea," Lily said. "Have a good time." She smiled sweetly.

"It was such a delicious supper, Lily," Jacob said. "Thank you very much." He looked at each couple in the room. "It was lovely to have met you all." He smiled. "I hope to see you in the future." He nodded and took Anna's hand in his, leading her through the dining room and outside.

The evening was beautiful. The sun had already set. The wind didn't ruffle even a leaf on the trees. It was a perfect night for a late walk under the stars. Jacob continued to hold

Anna's hand as they walked down the street away from their hosts' house. Beautiful maple trees lined the path on which they walked. In the distance they could hear music coming from the local hotel.

"Wouldn't it be wonderful if life were always this enchanting?" Jacob commented. "We could be together every minute of the day." He smiled down at Anna.

"It would be heavenly." Anna gazed up at Jacob. Jacob stopped and turned to Anna. He put his arms around her as they stood under a maple tree.

"If my carpentry business is prosperous," Jacob began to say, "I will build my own house on the little hill north of Abbington Pickets."

"Won't that be grand?" Anna exclaimed. "Will it be a big mansion like the Howards'?"

"Bigger!" Jacob played along. "I will have many maids, and many butlers."

"Wow! How many carriages shall you have?" Anna joked.

"At least six, maybe more." Jacob laughed.

"And will it have an indoor bathroom?" Anna's eyebrows lifted with a devilish smile on her face. "I am tired of going to the outhouse in the middle of the night."

"Of course," Jacob teased. "Anything you want."

"Well, just remember the little people." Anna giggled.

"I won't forget about you." Jacob stopped joking. "You will be there, right alongside me."

"Promise?" Anna asked softly.

"Promise," Jacob said with a smile.

"Look!" Jacob pointed to the sky above the trees. "Northern lights! They are out dancing tonight."

"Wow! They are beautiful tonight, aren't they?" Anna stared up at the sky. The beautiful green shades of aurora borealis danced through the sky. Jacob and Anna stood watching for several minutes in silence.

"I guess we better get back to Lily and David's," Jacob said, realizing that it was getting late. "Morning will come sooner than we think."

"When you're right, you're right," Anna agreed. Jacob slipped her hand back into his for the walk back. It felt so wonderful to be close to Anna. Jacob never wanted to let her go.

By the time Jacob and Anna reached the house the company had all gone home. Lily and David were in the sitting room enjoying a cup of tea before bed. "Would you two like a cup of tea?" Lily asked as she began to stand up to get it.

"No, thank you, Lily," both Jacob and Anna said simultaneously.

"Time for bed," Jacob said. "We have a long way to go in the morning."

"Did you two have a good walk?" she asked.

"Yes, thank you," Anna said. "The northern lights were out, and they are amazing."

"I don't think I have ever seen them quite as beautiful as they were tonight," Jacob added.

"We should have gone for a walk too, dear." Lily looked at David. Everyone laughed.

"Thank you again for that lovely supper," Jacob said.

"Yes, thank you," Anna agreed.

"My wife is a beautiful cook." David's compliment made his wife blush.

"Good night," Jacob said as he nodded to David and Lily.

"Good night, Jacob and Anna," Lily and David said.

Morning came sooner than Jacob would have liked. He and Anna had breakfast with the Adairs. Then he hitched up the horses and got ready for the journey back. Jacob had so much to think about and he was thrilled with his news. He didn't know how he was going to sleep at the stopping house tonight.

"Thank you so much for coming, Jacob." David shook his hand. "I will look forward to seeing more tables next month."

"Thank you, sir," Jacob said. "It's my pleasure."

"I will contact you with the driver details for the next delivery," David informed him.

Jacob drove the horses to the front of the house, where Anna and Lily waited with the luggage. Jacob hopped off to load the bags into the back of the wagon. "I made you enough lunch for the ride back," Lily told Jacob.

"That is wonderful," Jacob said gratefully. "Thank you very much."

"Yes," Anna said. "Thank you for your hospitality. You have a beautiful home."

"Thank you, my dear." Lily hugged her. "It was our pleasure."

Jacob shook David's hand and gave Lily a quick hug.

"Thank you, again," he said. He helped Anna into the wagon and then climbed in himself. David and Lily stood with their arms around each other, waving good-bye. Jacob and Anna waved as they drove away. They trotted along Main Street, meeting other teams of horses and slowing down for people crossing the street. All the hustle and bustle of the bigger town was too much for Jacob.

"I sure am glad we live in a nice, quiet, little village," Jacob commented as they drove through town. "I couldn't stand all this hustle and bustle everyday. I like my peace and quiet."

"I agree," Anna declared. "I like our charming little village." She smiled.

"Anna, I was serious," Jacob started. "I will build that house on the hill. I will succeed as a carpenter," he said with sincerity.

"I know." Anna looked over at Jacob. "You will be amazing. I have no doubt."

Jacob reached over and put his hand gently over hers.

"You will be there with me," Jacob said wholeheartedly.

"Of course I will," Anna agreed. "I live practically across the street." Anna laughed.

"No." Jacob tried to convey his seriousness to her. "You *really* will be with me."

"What do you mean?" Anna looked confused.

"I mean..." Jacob tried to finish his explanation. By this time, they were already travelling in the country. The big town of Kingston was behind them. Jacob abruptly pulled on the reins. "Whoa," he commanded the horses to stop.

"What are you doing?" asked Anna. "Why are you slowing down?" she questioned as Jacob completely stopped the horses and stood up and jumped off the wagon. He walked around to Anna's side and held out his hand to her. She held it and climbed off the wagon.

"What's this about?" she asked, with a worried look on her face. "What's the matter?"

Jacob stood in front of Anna, with her hand still in his. He dropped down to one knee and looked into her eyes. Anna gasped, putting her other hand to her mouth to cover it, and took a deep breath. "Anna," Jacob started, "you are an amazing girl." Jacob was so scared of what he was about to ask Anna. "You are beautiful, kind, thoughtful, and I can't imagine my life without you." Jacob cleared his throat. "Will you marry me?"

Jacob held his breath and closed his eyes. He was worried that her answer would be no. He quickly glanced up and saw her face light up. Her beautiful red lips were smiling. "I will!" she exclaimed. Jacob jumped to his feet and wrapped his arms around her waist and twirled her around and around. Then he stopped and stood still, looking at Anna. They were both almost too dizzy to stand up.

"You have made me the happiest man alive," Jacob exclaimed. "It won't always be easy, but I promise I will make you so happy."

"Oh, Jacob," Anna beamed. "You already make me happy." Jacob hugged her with all he had. He had always known, even when he was growing up, that marriage couldn't be taken lightly. The person he chose to marry was the one he intended to be with for the rest of his life.

"Make your choice wisely," his mother had once told him.

"I will ask your Pa, proper-like," Jacob stated. "I want to do this right. I don't want anything to ruin our happiness." Still smiling from ear to ear, they climbed back up on the wagon and started on their way. It didn't matter how much time it was going to take to get home; as long as Jacob was with Anna nothing else mattered.

The stay at the stopping house was uneventful this time, so they both had a good night's sleep. They were back in Abbington Pickets by the next evening. Jacob and Anna still couldn't stop smiling. They knew that they were going to spend the rest of their lives together.

chapter seventeen

Since Jacob and Anna had arrived back in Abbington Pickets the previous month, they had kept quite busy. Jacob immediately started working on the tables for David Adair in Kingston. After Jacob had asked Anna's father for her hand in marriage, she spent her time planning for their wedding in the spring. Anna also spent time with her Aunt Clara, south of Abbington, who helped her get started sewing her wedding dress.

Jacob was in his third week of helping the Rodgers with their harvest. They were shorthanded this year, and he was happy to oblige. Truth was, he missed them a lot. Not that he wasn't happy living in Abbington. On the contrary, he loved it. He just missed their parental guidance and unconditional love. While he was there, they never spoke of Abigail. Jacob knew that her wedding was coming up very soon. It was the second of October, to be exact. He remembered the date well, from her letter. He also knew that Mr. and Mrs. Rodgers weren't going, since the doctor had said that Mr. Rodgers' heart condition meant they should not travel that far.

Jacob's heart still ached for Abigail, and knowing that her wedding was approaching made him feel sad in a lonely way. That feeling was something he couldn't share with anyone. He knew first love hurt the worst and was the hardest to forget. Jacob's mama had told him when he was fourteen years old, "Your first love is the one love you take with you until you are no longer here on this earth to remember it." He had always wondered if she was speaking from experience. He had never asked her, and now he would never know. He thought it must be true, though, because he thought of that quote when he envisioned Abigail. He knew that he truly loved Anna but there would always be a special place in his heart for Abigail.

"Well, my boy," Mr. Rodgers exclaimed over supper with all the crew. "Harvest will be finished for another year after tomorrow."

"Yes, sir," agreed Jacob. He continued to eat the wonderful roasted chicken that Mrs. Rodgers had prepared.

"What are your plans for the winter?" Mr. Rodgers asked.

"I have a big continuous order for tables," Jacob started to explain. "Mr. Adair's brother is selling them in Kingston."

"Good for you, son," Mr. Rodgers said. "Mrs. Rodgers also tells me you are getting married."

"Yes, sir," Jacob said proudly, with a blushing smile.

"We wish you and Anna all the best," Mr. Rodgers said as he looked over at his wife. Mrs. Rodgers nodded and wiped the tears from her eyes. She was always so emotional about things of that sort.

"Thank you." Jacob didn't know what else to say. He was feeling the loss of his second family. They were just like parents to him.

"Glad you came to help, Jacob," Bert put in. "I am so happy things are working out for you in Abbington Pickets."

"Things couldn't be better." Jacob smiled. "My business is starting to take off. I am marrying the most wonderful girl in the world, and life is good." Jacob tried not to brag, but he was extremely blessed, and he felt like shouting it to the world.

"Just think," Bert added, "if you hadn't moved to Abbington Pickets, you wouldn't have your own business and I wouldn't be working for these fine folks, and my Alice wouldn't be here with us right now." Bert looked over at his new bride. He had picked her up from the train station in Kingston a few weeks ago. They were married in Kingston before Bert brought her to Goldenrod. Now she worked for Mrs. Rodgers, helping her with the housework, cooking, baking, and sewing. Alice was a petite young lady with dark brown hair pinned neatly in a loose bun. Her very dark eyebrows set off her green eyes. She was a soft-spoken, delicate lady, who looked at Bert with love in her eyes. It was apparent they were very much in love.

"That's right," Jacob agreed as he got up from his chair and walked over to Mrs. Rodgers. He hugged her tightly and said, "but I still miss this young lady." Mrs. Rodgers blushed and smiled at Jacob's compliment. "Well, I better get home," Jacob said. "I will be back bright and early tomorrow."

"You bet," Mr. Rodgers agreed. "It may have been a dry, hot year, but that sure made for a fast harvest season." Mr. Rodgers was right. The winter had not brought as much snow as usual, so it had been a dry spring. Then there were only a few rainstorms during the summer, which had made it a very dry season.

The ride home seemed long because Jacob was tired. He just wanted to get some sleep. His horse loped along at a steady pace, which made for a drowsy ride. However, Jacob still had a lot on his mind. He thought about constructing the tables for David, the wedding, and possibly building a house of their own right after the wedding. It was a good thing Jacob had a lot of tables started, or he might have been behind, helping Mr. Rodgers with harvest. Every morning he had gotten up extra early to work for an hour on them before he left for Goldenrod Ranch.

It was a beautiful calm night and the sun was setting as he rode toward the west. Once he reached Abbington and arrived at his place, he climbed off his horse in a daze. He led his horse to her stall, gave her water and oats, and went into his house.

"Hello, Jacob." A sweet voice came from the kitchen of his one room abode.

"Anna," Jacob said with surprise. "It's so good to see you." Jacob took her in his arms and hugged her close.

"I know it's late," Anna started to explain, "but we haven't seen each other much since you've been harvesting. I just had to see you before I went to sleep tonight."

"You don't have to explain, my sweet girl." Jacob soothed her as he stroked her hair with his hand. "I am delighted to see you."

"I won't stay long," she continued. "I told Pa I was just bringing you some cookies." She said this with a smile and a twinkle in her eye.

"Oh, really," Jacob said, "so where are these cookies," he teased, figuring she had used that as an excuse for her father and hadn't really brought him any.

"Right on the table over there, Sir Jacob," Anna joked.

"Well, I have been proven wrong again," Jacob laughed. "I better wash up. My clothes are full of grain dust and straw."

"Oh, I don't care," Anna said. "I just wanted to be near you."

"I will make you itchy," he smiled. "Don't say I didn't warn you." Jacob let go of Anna and walked over to his dresser. He turned his back toward Anna so she could only see the back of him, if she was looking. Jacob unbuttoned his shirt and took it off and threw it in his laundry basket. Jacob had well-developed muscle structure on his back and biceps. He quickly took a clean shirt out of his dresser and put it on and buttoned it up.

Anna walked over to him and put her arms around him from behind. "I can't wait until we are man and wife," she whispered. It was all Jacob could do to control his desire for her. He finished tucking his shirt in before he turned around to face her. Jacob put his rough, hard-working hands on her cheeks and held her head in his hands.

"Anna. You mean more to me than you will ever know," Jacob said gently. Anna closed her eyes as if Jacob was going to kiss her. "I would love to kiss you right now," Jacob continued, holding her. "I would desperately love to touch you right now." The tone of his voice was deep and smooth. "But I respect you too much."

Anna's face looked disappointed but then she smiled. "I love you, Jacob," she said, mesmerized by his words.

"I love you too, Anna." Jacob kissed her forehead and then let her go. His whole body screamed yes but his head and heart said no.

"Why don't we have some of those cookies," Jacob suggested, trying to change the subject.

"I'll make some tea," Anna agreed. "It will be a nice ending to a perfect evening." She smiled as she picked up the kettle, poured water into it, and set it on the stove.

Jacob sat at the table in his usual chair and Anna put the cookies on a plate. It didn't seem long until the kettle whistled. She poured the boiling water into the teapot along with the tea.

"It's a perfect evening, coming home to you." Jacob winked at Anna. "This is what it will be like come spring."

"Won't it be wonderful, Jacob!" Anna exclaimed with excitement.

"Maybe we should be moving that date up," Jacob joked.

"You're so funny." Anna laughed and ignored his suggestion.

"These cookies are the best," Jacob said with a smile.

"Jacob," Anna said sternly, "you have been saying that since I met you! Sometimes I think you only love me for my cookies!" She burst out laughing.

"Oh, no," Jacob laughed. "The secret's out! I guess we better not get married," he teased.

"Jacob Hudson," Anna scolded, "You take that back!" She pretended to pout.

Jacob couldn't help himself and continued to tease her until she was mad, but he knew it wouldn't last long. She was just playing along.

"Well, sunshine." Anna got up from her chair. "I better get going and let you get some sleep." Jacob stood up and walked her to the door.

"Let me walk you home," Jacob said with concern.

"I have walked in the dark before, handsome," Anna reassured him with a smile. Jacob grabbed his coat and handed Anna her shawl. He unlatched the door and proceeded to walk with her. Jacob put his arm around her as they walked toward her house.

"You're too good to me," Anna declared. "You will spoil me."

"Aww, you're worth it." Jacob smiled. "Just wait until we're married." They reached Anna's house and Jacob turned to Anna at the front doorstep. He gave her a kiss on the forehead and another quick hug.

"Harvest will be done tomorrow," Jacob said, "and then we can spend more time together."

"That's good to hear," Anna replied. "I'm going to my Aunt Clara's tomorrow. We're still working on designing my wedding dress."

"Have a good time," Jacob told her. "I will miss you." He stepped backward, moving slowly away from her, not wanting to leave.

"Good-bye, Jacob." Anna smiled as she waved to him.

"Good-bye." Jacob waved back and stepped into the darkness to walk back home.

Daylight came too quickly for Jacob's liking, because of his late night with Anna. *It was worth it,* Jacob thought to himself as he brushed one of the finished tables with a coat of varnish. It would be finished before he left for Goldenrod.

After washing his brush, he saddled his horse and galloped toward the ranch. By the time he got there, Mr. Rodgers, Bert, and the other neighbours were gathered by the threshing machine and almost ready to start. The day was warmer than was usual for that time of year. There was not a cloud in the sky to give any reprieve. Jacob and Bert took turns throwing stooks into the threshing machine. It was hard work. Jacob's sweat seeped through his shirt, under his arms, and down his back. The others were the same. The morning seemed to go by slowly with the exhausting heat of the sun. When dinner time came, they were all more than happy to stop.

"Whew!" Jacob took off his hat off and wiped his brow. "This is going to be a long day," he said to Bert. He was trying not to complain.

"I bet I drank three quarts of water," Bert responded.

The walk to the house was a slow one. Mrs. Rodgers had dinner on the table, along with a huge pitcher of water and tea. No matter how hot the weather, the English would still drink tea! Jacob chuckled out loud at the thought.

"What's so funny, lad?" Bert asked with a curious look on his face.

"Nothing," Jacob answered with a smile still on his face.

"Come on," Bert insisted, "it has to be something or you wouldn't be laughing."

"It's hotter than hell itself today and you English still want to drink tea!" Jacob exclaimed.

"So, you find that funny, lad?" Bert questioned with a smirk.

"Well, I find it crazy," Jacob joked.

"It does sound a little crazy," Bert admitted. "But did you know that when you put hot liquid in your body it actually cools you down?"

"I don't believe you." Jacob thought Bert was kidding.

"It's true!" Bert insisted.

"Boys, boys," Mrs. Rodgers said. "What are you arguing about?"

"Just tea in the summertime," Jacob laughed.

"Tea is good anytime," she replied.

"It's too hot for tea," Jacob pointed out.

"Tea cools you down on a hot day," she declared.

"See, see, see! What did I tell you, lad?" Bert looked satisfied with himself.

"I still can't believe it." Jacob shook his head in disbelief. The petty little argument came to an abrupt halt with the sound of the door slamming and someone running into the dining room yelling at the top of his lungs.

"Fire! Fire! Fire!" It was Michael, one of the neighbour's boys, who was helping with the harvest.

"What?" yelled Mr. Rodgers. "Where? Outside?" Everyone stood up at once and ran out the doorway to see where the fire was. To the southwest was a cloud of heavy, thick, black smoke stretched out for miles.

"Prairie fire!" Jacob yelled as he ran for his horse. The others followed behind.

"That's really close to Abbington!" yelled Mr. Rodgers.

"Anna!" Jacob cried out loud. *I have to get to her*, he thought to himself. "Get the wagon and load the plow," he ordered

Bert and Michael. He mounted and galloped away as fast as his horse could take him.

"Be careful!" Mrs. Rodgers hollered after him. She stood at the front door feeling helpless as a lamb.

"Hee-ya!" The voices of the eleven other men leaving the yard rang out. The only sound left in the air was the horses' hooves pounding.

Jacob galloped his horse as fast as she could go. Adrenaline was kicking in. He didn't feel how hot the weather was now. All he could think about was getting to Anna.

The wind seemed to have picked up since morning, and it pushed the fire along even faster. It seemed to be moving north. *How did this fire start? Where is it, exactly? Who would be crazy enough to start a fire this time of year?* These thoughts ran through Jacob's mind as the hot breeze burned his face. The fire was still south of Abbington Pickets. *What a relief!* Jacob thought to himself, *Anna would be safe.* They needed to stop the fire before it burned any further. After galloping for two miles, Jacob reached a farmer, who was already plowing a furrow in his field, trying to make a fire guard to stop the fire. Jacob galloped up to the farmer.

"What can I do to help?" he yelled from a distance.

"Here, take this. I'll get my other plow." The farmer held the reins out to Jacob so he could take over. Jacob hopped off his horse and the farmer climbed on and galloped toward the barn. Jacob continued to plow the field. The smoke blew in his face. With one hand he grabbed his hanky from his pocket and covered his nose and mouth to keep from breathing it. There was so much smoke blowing past him. It stung his eyes and took his breath away despite his efforts to cover his mouth. The fire was getting closer and he was now plowing adjacent to it. He could see another person plowing next to him, and one beyond him. That was as far as he could see, because the smoke was so thick. They needed to stop this fire from getting any further or it would destroy all the neighbouring crops.

If only it hadn't been so dry this fall, Jacob thought. His heart beat with fear at the thought of the fire wiping out Abbington Pickets, and all the families who lived there.

Hours had passed, with fifty or more men plowing furrows for miles to try to keep the fire from burning further. They needed to save the crops, and, most of all, the village of Abbington Pickets. The wind had died down and as the fire reached the fire guard it slowed down. Jacob and the other men were exhausted. Their faces were black from smoke. Jacob could hear men coughing and coughing in the distance. He looked up and noticed that the sky had grown dark. It looked like rain.

"Praise the Lord; rain is coming!" Jacob pointed to the sky and yelled to everyone. He could hear cheers in the distance. It was quite a sight to see that many men scattered in the distance over the fields. The farmer's wife walked out to the fields with fresh water for everyone to drink. She walked over to each man and gave him a drink. The men continued to plow. The fire wasn't out yet, and this wasn't the time to stop; it could leap to life without a moment's notice if the wind started up again. It would only take seconds for the flames to be in full force once again.

Just then a loud crack of thunder came from the sky. A few minutes later the clouds opened and huge raindrops fell, like gifts from heaven. "Yaaaayyyy!" Jacob and the other men cheered simultaneously. Jacob was so relieved. He could go home and see Anna. The crops were saved and Abbington was preserved. Exhaustion started to set in as Jacob and the other men pulled the plows up into the farmer's yard. Each one took their horses for a drink of well-deserved water and fed them hay and oats. The horses were as tired as the men. They had also worked to their limits.

Jacob spotted Bert and Mr. Rodgers as they walked toward him. Mr. Rodgers was coughing. "You shouldn't even be here,

Mr. Rodgers," Jacob said, concerned about his heart condition. "You better get back to the house with Bert."

"I'm alright, my boy," Mr. Rodgers told him. He covered his mouth with his hankie and coughed again. "Take him home," Jacob directed Bert. Bert nodded in agreement, and Jacob tied Mr. Rodgers's horse to the wagon.

"Here, let me help you," Jacob said as he held Mr. Rodgers's hand and helped him step up to the wagon seat.

"I will come by tomorrow, Mr. Rodgers," he told him. "See you, Bert." It was still raining but no one seemed to mind getting wet. It felt good to be cool again. Just as they were about to leave, the farmer walked over to their wagon.

"Thank you so much for your help." He spoke to everyone there. "I don't know what I would have done without you."

"No problem, sir," Jacob said. "Happy to help, and glad we were able to keep Abbington Pickets safe too."

"I just saw that fire coming toward my field," the man stated. "I don't know how it started. All I know is it travelled fast."

"It's unbelievable how fast a fire can go," Jacob added.

"I believe it came from the farm east of the Howards'," the farmer stated.

Jacob stood holding his reins. He just wanted to get going. He was anxious to see Anna and hold her in his arms after such a stressful ordeal. Jacob climbed up onto his horse.

"Take care," he told the farmer, and waved to Bert and Mr. Rodgers in the distance. He started toward Abbington. It was only another mile away.

As Jacob slowly rode home, the smell of smoke welled up in his nostrils. The sight of burnt crops and grass stretched on for miles and patches still smouldered. *Thank the Lord for the rain,* Jacob thought, *or more damage might have been done.* Jacob was in a daze as he got closer to Abbington. As he remembered what the farmer had said: "I think it started east of the Howards'," Jacob suddenly came wide awake and realized Anna had gone to her Aunt Clara's today. She lived near there.

"Hee-ya!" Jacob yelled to his horse and they picked up speed almost immediately. Jacob leaned forward to ride as fast as they could travel. The rain slapped his face and the wind blew his hair back. He prayed that Anna was home safe and sound, that she had changed her mind and had not gone to her aunt's today. He had visions of her sitting on the porch watching the rain falling.

He entered Abbington Pickets and raced down Main Street, straight to Anna's house. His horse stopped and he quickly jumped off and ran to the house. He yanked open the door. "Anna! Anna! Anna!" he yelled. He looked in every corner of the one-room house. No one, not even her father, was there. Jacob ran across the street to the blacksmith shop. He threw open the door but there wasn't anyone there either. *Maybe she's at my place,* he thought to himself. He climbed back on his horse and raced down the street behind the hotel. He rushed into his house but there was no sign of Anna, just an empty room. Jacob's heart pounded hard. He felt like it was going to jump right out of his chest. He grabbed his reins, put his foot in the stirrup and pulled himself up into his saddle. He looked up and saw someone drive by in a horse and wagon whom he recognized. They were driving slowly down the street, headed west. He dropped the reins and ran over to the wagon.

"Whoa." The driver stopped his horse when he saw Jacob running toward him.

"Jacob." Anna's father jumped off the wagon, trying to stop Jacob. His face was black from smoke. It was obvious that his hands were badly burned. His face was tear-stained and his clothes were torn and had burn holes in the sleeves. He reached Jacob and looked into his eyes without saying a word. Jacob looked past him at the wagon. He could see something, covered with blankets, in the back.

"Anna!" Jacob yelled as he darted toward the wagon. His hands stretched out to grab what was inside. Anna's father held Jacob's arms to keep him from getting any closer. He struggled to get free, but the blacksmith was stronger than Jacob.

"Let me go!" Jacob screamed. "Let me go." Jacob's emotions flooded his body and tears streamed down his face. He fought to get free. He didn't want to believe that Anna was gone. Jacob fell to his knees, sobbing. With his work-beaten hands, he grabbed a handful of grass and ripped it from the ground. He screamed as he threw it, "Noooooooo!" He curled forward as he sat on his knees, while the rain poured down on him. He repeated over and over, "Not my Anna. Not my Anna."

Anna's father tried to calm Jacob down, but he was dealing with his own grief. Not only had he lost his only daughter, he had also lost his sister, a niece, and a nephew.

The fire had been near their home and they feared it would burn their farm. They were in danger. They tried to run to the neighbours for safety. The wind came up and they didn't have a chance. The fire had swept right over them. When the blacksmith found them, he saw that his sister had lain over her children to try to save them. Anna lay beside her aunt, holding her hand.

Anna's father left and Mr. Adair tried to get Jacob up and out of the rain. "Son, you need to come into the house," he coaxed him. Jacob stood up. His head was pounding from the tears he had shed. His mind was racing a mile a minute, and he felt like he was waking up from a nightmare.

Mr. Adair took Jacob to his home, and his wife made them both a plate of supper and some coffee. "I don't feel like eating," Jacob said, staring into thin air as he sat at the kitchen table. His body was there but he didn't seem to be.

Jacob felt numb. He had no feeling left. He thought that all his emotions had died with Anna. *How could God let this happen?* He felt so angry with God at that moment. God had taken every person he loved dearly, starting with Lucy. *Why?* he screamed inside his head.

chapter eighteen

Weeks had passed since that horrific day in September. Jacob hadn't left his house. He sat in his chair and didn't care if he lived or died. His haggard appearance would have scared a child. He hadn't shaved or changed his clothes for weeks. Between Mr. Adair bringing food and Mrs. Rodgers sending food everyday, Jacob shouldn't have gone hungry, but he wouldn't eat. They were really good to him. Even Bert came to check on him. Charles stopped by a few times to see if there was anything he could do, but Jacob didn't have much to say. Sometimes there were knocks at the door; Jacob would ignore them.

Sleep wasn't his friend these days. When he laid his head down to rest, all he could see was Anna's smiling face. More than not he was wakened by his usual nightmare of Lucy calling for him.

"Hello? Hello?" Someone had opened the door a crack. "Jacob, are you here?" It was Mrs. Rodgers. She walked in and found Jacob sitting in his usual place at the table, staring at the wall. "Jacob, dear." She spoke softly and sympathetically when she saw him in this state. "Mr. Rodgers told me it was bad." She looked around the room, with dishes piled up, laundry lying on the floor, and garbage overflowing the wastebasket; not to mention Jacob in need of a clean shirt and a shave. She pulled up a chair across from Jacob and held his hands in hers. "Jacob? Are you listening to me?" she asked.

"I don't care anymore," Jacob said plainly. "When I care, it's just taken away from me."

"Oh, Jacob, that's not true." She tried to console his heavy heart. "Time heals a broken heart."

"Not this time," he said with no emotion.

Mrs. Rodgers leaned over and wrapped her arms around Jacob and held him close. His head rested on her chest. He began to cry softly.

"There, there." She stroked his hair. "Let it all out." Jacob sobbed for several minutes while she held him. All he could feel was anguish and nothing could make it better. Mrs. Rodgers let go of Jacob and stood up. "Now," she looked around, "I am going to do a little cleaning around here." She started by picking up the dirty clothes from the floor. "I will take these home to wash," she said.

"You don't have to do anything." Jacob wiped his eyes, still sitting in his chair.

"Oh, yes, I do," she said firmly. "You are going to take a bath and have a shave."

"I don't feel like it. I just want to be left alone," Jacob stated.

"Well, that isn't going to happen." It was obvious that she was trying tough love and it hurt her dearly to speak to Jacob this way. He was like a son to her; it broke her heart to see him this way. She went outside with a pail to get some water from the well. When she got back, she put it on the stovetop to heat for Jacob's bath. Jacob didn't seem to care one way or the other. He sat at the table while she worked around him.

"I have prepared the tub for you in the kitchen," Mrs. Rodgers told him. "Go get undressed and get in." She said it almost like she was talking to a five-year-old. Jacob was hesitant, since this was a one-room house, and there was nowhere to go without her seeing him naked. "Don't worry, I won't look at you," she added. "I will find you some clean clothes."

Jacob slowly walked over to the tub. He hesitantly unbuttoned his dirty shirt and took it off. Then he dropped it on the floor. He unbuttoned his britches and kicked them off and left them on the floor as well. He lifted his leg and dipped his foot in the water to check the temperature. It felt pleasing, so he climbed into the tub one foot at a time and sat down. The hot water felt good, he had to admit, but didn't change the fact that he was mourning the loss of his love.

Jacob bathed in a daze. He didn't take long washing himself. Then he stood up, climbed out, dried off, and put on the clean clothes Mrs. Rodgers had set on the table for him. She changed the bed sheets while he finished up with a shave.

"Don't you feel much better?" Mrs. Rodgers asked, as she touched his arm in a caring way. Jacob walked over to his freshly-made bed and sat down. He hung his head down and looked at the floor. Thoughts of Anna came rushing to his mind. He didn't want to think about it anymore. He just wanted the pain to go away. Mrs. Rodgers sat down on the bed next to him and took his hand in hers.

"Jacob," she started, "I know you are hurting, but believe me when I tell you it won't last forever." The concern on her face made Jacob feel as though she could possibly be right.

"I just want to close my eyes," Jacob said, "and wake up to Anna's beautiful face." Tears welled up in his eyes and bitterness began to throb in his heart.

"I wish it were that easy, Jacob," she comforted him.

Knock, knock sounded from the door as Mr. Rodgers entered Jacob's living quarters.

"Good day, Jacob," he began. "How are you doing today?" He held his hat in his hands.

Jacob lifted his tear-stained face and looked at Mr. Rodgers. "Could be better, sir," Jacob answered.

"Well, are you ready, dear?" Mrs. Rodgers asked Mr. Rodgers.

"Yes, I got everything I needed in Abbington," he replied. "Best be getting home to do the chores." Mrs. Rodgers gathered her shawl and her belongings, along with Jacob's dirty laundry.

"Jacob, there is a plate of supper for you in the icebox," she reminded him. "Please eat something." She hugged him gently.

"If you need anything, we are here for you, Jacob," Mr. Rodgers told him. Jacob looked at him and nodded. The sadness in his eyes was undeniable.

"Jacob, I wish you would come and stay with us," Mrs. Rodgers said with a worried face. "At least until you're back on your feet." All Jacob could do was shake his head. "I am praying for you." She smiled.

"Good-bye son," Mr. Rodgers said. "Take care of yourself." He patted Jacob on the back and they left. Jacob walked over to his bed, pulled back the covers, and crawled between the sheets. He covered himself up and closed his eyes. Many thoughts swirled in his mind, and he tried to block them out by going to sleep. First it was Anna smiling at him and bringing him cookies, then Abigail trying to kiss him when she was intoxicated, and finally his mama kissing his cheek and telling him he was a good boy. At last he dozed off.

"Jacob! Jacob! Jacob!" the voice inside his head said over and over. Instantly Jacob sat straight up in bed. He remembered his familiar dream all too well. Sweat on his brow, his heart pounding, Jacob jumped out of bed, grabbing his coat from the hanger on the wall beside the door as he walked outside. It was dark by that time, and there were not very many people around at that time of night.

He could hear music coming from inside the Empire Hotel. It was still in full swing by the sound of it. He couldn't see much because the door was closed, but he could hear piano music and quite a lot of laughter. Jacob walked up the steps to the hotel door and put his hand on the latch. He stood there for a moment. *This wasn't a place for him,* he told himself, but where could he go when he felt as terrible as he did? *Remember what happened the last time you stepped foot in here,* he reminded himself. Of course, that brought Anna to mind, front and centre, and with that he proceeded to open the door.

Cigar smoke filled the room and there were a lot of people walking about. Jacob walked up to the bar and sat down. He leaned against the counter. The room wasn't exactly full. In fact, there weren't as many people here as it had sounded like from outside. Jacob saw two men playing a game of pool, three guys playing darts in the opposite corner, and four well-dressed men playing poker. It was only Jacob and the gentleman beside him at the bar.

"What'll you have?" the bartender asked.

"Uh well, I didn't..." Jacob tried to speak.

"Alright, what do you think this is?" the bartender said angrily. "You don't drink, you know where the door is." He gestured in the direction Jacob had come from.

"I'll have what he's having," Jacob said, pointing at the gentleman beside him. It was the first of many drinks that night.

Jacob woke up with a pounding headache. He looked around but didn't remember anything since his first drink. He realized he was in his own bed but he wasn't sure how he had got there. Jacob realized that he hadn't experienced the nightmare, nor had he thought about Anna or Abigail, or even his mother, all night. For the first time since Anna had died, he had slept without being abruptly awakened. It was the first time he had forgotten his anguish. Jacob's head started to clear, revealing the reality that Anna was dead, Abigail was gone, and his life over.

Night after night Jacob spent in the hotel. One day ran into another. He didn't know what time of day it was, or what day of the week it was. Drinking was a way of passing the time without recollecting the truth. Unbeknownst to Jacob, when the Empire Hotel closed, he would stagger to his own bed and fall into a deep sleep. Days turned into weeks of inebriation for Jacob. His tall frame looked weak from loss of weight. Mr. Adair knocked on his door every day, to no avail. David Adair came from Kingston to inquire about the tables Jacob agreed to build for him. Two months had passed without a shipment and David was wondering about his order. Not because he needed the tables for sales, but out of concern for Jacob's well-being.

It was known around the village that Jacob was spending a lot of time in the hotel, and that he wasn't coping well after Anna's death. Mrs. Rodgers often went to his house and cleaned and made meals for him. Even Charles came over from time to time. But not even Anna's father could get through to him. Besides drinking in the saloon, Jacob did nothing to enhance his life. He thought time and time again that he would rather die than live another day without Anna.

One sunny winter Sunday after church, Bert stopped by to check on Jacob. Jacob didn't answer the door. As usual, he just let Bert knock. Bert knew enough to come in without an invitation. "Jacob, lad," Bert said cheerily. "How are you doing?" Jacob was still in bed with the covers almost over his head. Bert pretended he was up and talked to him in his usual manner.

Jacob moaned at the disruption of his sleep. It was much earlier than he was used to getting up now. "Come on, lad." Bert shook the bed. "Time for tea."

"Oh, go away," Jacob snapped. "No time is a good time for tea." Jacob was irritated, and was still slightly intoxicated.

"Oh, sure it is," Bert said. "Why, back home we would have had three pots by now," he joked. Bert walked over to the stove and added more wood. The place was quite cold, since Jacob had neglected to take care of the fire. Once Bert finished making the tea, he poured a cup for Jacob and placed it at his spot by the kitchen table.

"Lad, I think it's time you got up," Bert told him.

"I don't really feel like it." Jacob groaned some more.

"Well, sometimes we have to do things we don't like," Bert said sternly. "Come to the table and drink your tea."

"I never asked you to come here," Jacob raised his voice. "Why are you bothering me?" Jacob, in his mourning, didn't know what he was saying. Neither did he mean it. He didn't want to be angry at such a kind man as Bert. He was just so angry at the world, including God, that at that moment he didn't care what he said or to whom he said it.

"That's right," Bert declared loudly. "You didn't ask me here, but I am your friend. Where I come from, friends help one another. You may not realize it yet, but you really need a friend right now," Bert plainly said.

Jacob was taken aback. He had expected him to get mad and leave, so he could go back to sleep and be alone. Jacob was sorry that he had been short with his friend. *Obviously, Bert is a better friend than I am,* he thought.

Jacob put his head down in his hands. "I can't get Anna out of my mind." Tears welled up in his eyes. "I am so angry," he raised his voice.

"I know it's hard," Bert tried to console him, "but life goes on."

"How can I go on?" Jacob demanded. "The one person who made my life worth living is gone."

"Your life is worth living," Bert said. "God gave you a special gift. You must continue to use that gift."

"What are you talking about?" Jacob shouted. "God is just good at giving you something good and then ripping it from your grasp."

"Are you blaming God for Anna's death?" Bert asked.

"Well, why else did she die? And my sister Lucy? And my mother?" Jacob retorted angrily. "Every important person in my life, God took from me."

"God didn't take your Anna away from you, lad," Bert reassured him. "It's not God's purpose to destroy us. He loves all of us."

"It doesn't feel like it," Jacob said soberly.

"Man created that fire, not God. He gives us free will to accept it or be angry about it," Bert explained. "God loves you." Bert patted Jacob on the back.

"Why? That's all I can ask God," Jacob said. "I am so angry with Him right now."

"We don't always understand, but understanding comes through faith," Bert said. "We have to have faith in God, and let Him into our lives." Jacob started to understand what Bert was trying to say. His heart felt warm, as though peace blanketed his whole body.

"God wants you to come to Him," Bert told him. "He wants to heal your broken heart." Jacob fell down to his knees and started to cry. Bert crouched down with him on the floor, placed his hand on his back, and began to pray. "Lord Jesus, I pray for Jacob right now. He is hurting," Bert started, "Please heal his broken heart, and give him peace. May he come to know You, Lord." Jacob looked up with tears running down his face. He felt guilty for straying away from the Lord and being angry with Him.

"I am so sorry, Lord," he pleaded. "Please forgive me."

"Jacob, would you like to ask Jesus into your heart?" Bert asked. Jacob nodded. "Repeat after me," Bert instructed. "Lord Jesus, I thank you, Lord. I repent of my sins. Please come into my heart." Jacob repeated the words after Bert. "I make You Lord of my life. In Jesus' name. Amen."

Jacob looked at Bert with more kindness in his heart than he had felt when Bert arrived. "Thank you, Bert," Jacob said quietly. "I feel as though a heaviness has been lifted from me."

"Don't thank me, Jacob." Bert pointed upwards. "Thank the Lord Himself. You see, He will never leave you, nor forsake you. All you have to do is ask." Bert and Jacob stood up and walked over to the table and sat down.

"And Bert, thank you for not giving up on me," Jacob started, "I am sorry for how I treated you." He was ashamed of the way he had acted recently.

"It's forgotten, lad," Bert reassured him.

"Now, for that cup of tea." Bert smiled as he poured them each a cup.

"Thanks," Jacob said with a grin.

chapter nineteen

From the day Bert visited onward, Jacob didn't go to the hotel or take another drink. He now knew he could carry on with his life with God's help. Jacob started doing carpentry again, constructing tables in full swing. He made up for lost time. Jacob had ten tables built in the first week and he sent them to Kingston. Then he started the next ten.

Jacob visited all the people who helped him through his darkest moments. He apologized for treating them badly and acting the way he did. Mrs. Rodgers was so happy to see the smile back on his face. Mr. Adair was relieved that Jacob was back to his usual happy self, but realized there was something different about him. Jacob was peaceful and full of joy, more so than before. David and Lily were glad that tables were coming their way once again, but happier that Jacob was doing well.

It wasn't always easy. Jacob remembered Anna fondly, and he knew he would cherish her memory for the rest of his life. Going to church wasn't the same as it had been, and continuing his life without Anna was a day-to-day struggle. Daily prayer was part of his new routine; it gave him strength in ways he never thought possible. He knew God had a purpose for him and that there was someone special out there for him.

It was another hard winter. The snow drifted up past the windows. When the weather was good, Mr. and Mrs. Rodgers invited Jacob over for Sunday dinners after church. Jacob loved going to see them. They were the closest thing he had to parents, and he felt very loved when he was with them. Mrs. Rodgers never reminded Jacob of the day she had visited him and tried to get him back on his feet. He would never forget her nurturing kindness.

Jacob kept busy with his carpentry work, and helped Mr. Adair at The General Store when he needed help. Business was so prosperous that Jacob was able to start saving money to build his own house with a shop attached. Jacob couldn't believe that these small tables he built could make women so happy, and that he had built a successful business out of making them. It was all thanks to Mr. Adair, of course, and his brother, David.

Spring had sprung and it was an unusually warm, sunny day for that time of year. Jacob was cleaning ashes out of the stove when he heard a knock at the door. "Jacob," the voice said. "Are you home?"

"Yep," Jacob answered. "In here, Mr. Adair,"

"Can you work at the store for me today?" Mr. Adair asked, as he stood at the door.

"Of course." Jacob walked closer to the door, brushing the sawdust from his britches and shirt.

"I have some local deliveries to make," Mr. Adair explained. "It may take most of the day."

"No problem," Jacob reassured him. "I'll change my clothes and be over in a few minutes."

"Thanks, son." Mr. Adair stepped back out the doorway. "See you over there." He walked toward The General Store.

Jacob walked over to his bedroom quarters and changed into more suitable clothes for the job. He left his shop with a note on the door explaining that he would be next door if anyone needed anything. Jacob met Mr. Adair in front of

The General Store. He put on the apron Mr. Adair wore to protect his clothes and helped him load his wagon with the parcels he had to deliver.

"See you later." Mr. Adair waved to Jacob as he drove the wagon away from the store. Jacob had worked in the store before. Sometimes it wasn't very busy, so he would find things to do, like sweep the floor or the outside step and wooden sidewalk. It wasn't work he loved to do. He would rather be constructing something with his hands. Today, he had regular customers coming and going all morning, picking up groceries and whatnot. At one point, Jacob found himself alone in the store. He was putting away some cans of tomatoes on the shelf when the bell on the door alerted Jacob that someone had come in.

"Hello," Jacob spoke. He didn't know who he was speaking to, as he hadn't seen the person yet.

"Well. If it isn't the hero," a familiar voice said gruffly. Jacob recognized his father's voice, and cringed at the sound of it. He walked out from behind the shelf he was restocking and stood face to face with his father.

"Good afternoon, sir," Jacob said formally. He tried to forget that they were enemies, despite being father and son. He tried to pretend that he hadn't heard his father's rude comment.

"Mr. Adair trusts you to watch the store now," Pa sneered. "Well, I bet you think you're pretty smart."

"I'm just helping him out." Jacob ignored his comment. "Is there anything I can help you with?" He tried to change the subject.

"You would love that, wouldn't you? I'll wait until Adair is back," he stated plainly, and with that he turned around and walked out the doorway, putting his hat back on his head. Jacob walked to the window and watched his father climb up onto the wagon and holler at his horses, then drive off. It was apparent from the way he whipped his horses that he was aggravated. Jacob had noticed how much he had aged since his mother's funeral. His father had always treated his mother terribly, but they had been together for over twenty-five years and Jacob knew that deep down his father had loved her.

Jacob was left with a feeling of despair. *Why is my father so angry at me all the time?* he asked himself. It had been years since Jacob had left home. He couldn't believe his father had held a grudge that long.

Mr. Adair returned around three o'clock that afternoon with an empty wagon. Jacob was relieved to see him. He couldn't wait to go home and do some work he enjoyed. He loved helping Mr. Adair, but meeting his father had dampened his day. Jacob needed some time alone.

"I'll unhitch the horses for you, sir," Jacob offered.

"Thank you very much, Jacob." Mr. Adair appeared tired and was thankful for Jacob's help. He handed him the reins and went into the store. Jacob was happy to take the horses to the stable and unhitch them from the wagon. He fed and watered them, then put them in the shed for the rest of the day.

Jacob went back to the store to let Mr. Adair know what had happened during the day. "Hope it wasn't too much trouble for you," Mr. Adair said. "Were you busy with customers?" he asked.

"It wasn't a bad day," Jacob answered. He didn't want to tell him about the run-in with his father. "Mrs. Smyth stopped in for some flour and cinnamon," Jacob answered. "She must be making apple pie or cinnamon buns," he joked.

"Yep," Mr. Adair agreed. "She does bake a lot."

"Well, with nine kids," Jacob laughed, "you would be baking quite a bit too."

"You're right." Mr. Adair laughed along with Jacob.

"Well, I better get going," Jacob said as he took off the apron and handed it to Mr. Adair. "I have to get the stove stoked for supper."

"Why don't you join me and the Mrs. for supper tonight?" Mr. Adair suggested. "It's the least I can do to repay you for helping me out, especially on such short notice."

"I don't want to impose," Jacob answered, feeling a little shy.

"Oh, come on," Mr. Adair insisted. "Go do what you need to, and come to the house around six." He wasn't taking "no" for an answer.

"Alright," Jacob gave in with a smile. "See you at six." Jacob left the store and shut the door behind him. He walked off the step and started across the street, but stopped when he noticed a man on a horse racing toward him. As the man got closer, he saw it was his friend Charles. He could hear him yelling, but couldn't make out anything he was saying. He was still too far away. Confused by why his friend would be in such a hurry, he started to run toward him to see what the problem was. They got closer and Charles yelled, "It's your father!"

"What about him?" Jacob asked. He had just seen him earlier today. What could he possibly want after such an awful encounter? Charles jumped off his horse and stood in front of Jacob.

"He's had a terrible accident," Charles blurted out. "He's in bad shape."

"What kind of accident?" Jacob asked, confused. He grabbed Charles by the arms.

"He's asking for you, Jacob," Charles said earnestly.

"Me?" Jacob cried in disbelief. "Are you sure you know what you are saying?"

"Yes," Charles said soberly.

Jacob turned away to walk toward his house. "He doesn't want me." Charles followed after him with a desperate look on his face.

"Your brother sent for you." The serious look in Charles's eyes told Jacob that he wasn't fooling around this time.

Jacob stopped walking and said, "I just have to saddle up. Wait for me." He ran to the stable behind the hotel. Mr. Adair was outside.

"Sorry, Mr. Adair," Jacob yelled as he was going by, "I have to go." Jacob threw a saddle on his horse, cinched it up, and climbed on. They galloped toward Crocus Flats. Charles rode alongside him.

As they sped down the lane toward the stone house, Jacob noticed that the yard wasn't as neat and tidy as it used to be. The grass was overgrown. There were no flowers in the flower beds and some of the trees had died and needed to be chopped down. Jacob felt despair as he got closer to the homestead. He didn't know what he was going to see when he reached the house. Given the run-in with his father that very day, Jacob couldn't understand why he could possibly want to see him.

"Whoa," Jacob said to his horse as he pulled on the reins. The horse stopped and he quickly jumped off. Charles followed him. Jacob walked up the steps to the back door. He knocked. "Hello?" He opened the door and went in. He walked through the porch into the kitchen.

"Jacob!" Jane exclaimed as she ran up and hugged him. Her eyes looked swollen and red from crying. "I am so happy you're here."

"What's happened to Pa?" Jacob questioned her. "I just saw him in town this morning."

"It's awful, just awful," Jane declared as she cried into her apron.

"Jacob," Peter said as he and Andrew came down the stairs together, "Pa's in here. Come, he's asking for you."

"Can someone please tell me what happened?" Jacob demanded.

"Jane found him on the floor in the barn," Peter explained. "He was bleeding from a lot of wounds." Jane sobbed as Peter explained what had taken place.

"I saw the horses running around in the yard," Jane added. "I couldn't figure out what they were doing. I ran outside calling Pa. He didn't answer." Jane kept wiping her tears with her apron as she spoke. "I found him lying in one of the horse stalls, all curled up and bleeding." Jane couldn't help but sob uncontrollably with the recollection.

Jacob listened in horror.

"If I had only gotten there sooner." Jane cried harder. "If I had known he had come home." Peter tried to console Jane, and he held her while she cried.

"His horses trampled him, Jacob," Andrew stated plainly.

Jacob imagined what had happened. The stairs creaked as he walked up to the bedroom to see his father. He could see a pile of bloody rags in the laundry basket when he entered. His father was lying in his bed. He had a white rag wrapped around his forehead, and his arms were wrapped as well. He was covered in a quilt that his wife had made.

"Didn't someone send for Doc?" Jacob whispered to Andrew.

"He's been and gone," Andrew answered quietly. "Doc said to just make him comfortable." Andrew shook his head.

Jacob walked closer to his father. He could hardly recognize him because his face was so battered and bruised.

"Jacob?" His father muttered, half conscious. He tried to open his eyes.

"Yes, Pa." Jacob sat down on the chair next to the bed.

"Jacob?" he repeated.

"I am here," Jacob reassured him. His father tried to reach out to him with his bandaged arms and hands. He seemed to be getting worked up about something, but he couldn't speak very well and he was in a lot of pain.

"It's alright, Pa," Jacob said to him. "Just rest. I am here." Jacob sat by his side while he slept. Peter and Andrew left him there while they did the chores. Jane couldn't bring herself to see their father in that state. She stayed downstairs trying to keep busy with cooking and cleaning. Charles tried to help Jane; he didn't want to leave her alone. Sarah had not yet arrived. She was on her way from Kingston with her new husband.

"Come on, Jacob," Jane whispered from the hallway. "Supper is ready." Jacob stood up from the chair and walked out to the hallway.

"I'm not hungry," he said. "I don't want to leave him alone."

"But you have to eat," she insisted.

"I'm alright," he told her. He turned around and went back into the room and sat down.

"Jacob," his father said again as he stirred awake. "Son," was all he could say at that moment.

"I am here, Pa," Jacob said. "Save your energy."

"Son," he persisted, "I am sorry."

"It's alright, Pa." Jacob leaned closer to hear what Pa was saying.

"Listen," he whispered, barely able to talk. "Lucy." His breathing was becoming more laboured.

"What about Lucy?" Jacob asked. He moved closer to hear him better.

"I never meant to hurt her," he said.

"I know, Pa." Tears welled up in Jacob's eyes.

"I should have trained that horse better. I knew she wasn't ready for the field, but I used her anyway." He turned his head to hide his tears. "It's all my fault."

"No, Pa. No." Jacob tried to console him.

"I didn't know what else to do." He started to sob quietly. He wheezed and coughed, and his breathing became more laboured.

"It wasn't your fault, Pa."

"I know you were there."

Jacob was shocked by this confession. "Why didn't you say anything?" he questioned.

"I didn't know what to do." Pa cried harder. "Poor Lucy. I was so angry with her and then..." He didn't finish the sentence.

"Why didn't you tell Ma?" Jacob asked. "Losing Lucy just about killed her."

"I know, I know." Pa shook his head from side to side. "I am so sorry." He continued to sob.

Jacob felt anger building inside him. He remembered that day. "No one would have blamed you."

"I didn't want everyone to think that I had killed my own little girl." Pa's breathing was raspy and he coughed harder. "I didn't want you to tell," he confessed. "That's why I bullied you until you left."

"I don't understand," Jacob said, confused. "I didn't tell then; why would I have said anything later?"

"I wasn't thinking. I was scared, Jacob. I hated myself for letting it happen."

Jacob sobbed quietly as he listened to his father's confession. "I was angry at you for knowing." He gasped for air. "Oh, Lord, can you forgive me?" He spoke as if to the Heavens. "Can you ever forgive me, Jacob?" It was the first time that Jacob could remember his father treating him with respect and kindness.

"Of course, I forgive you." Jacob wiped his tears with his sleeve. He wanted to hug his father, but feared he would hurt him.

"I love you, son," he whispered, barely breathing.

That was all Jacob had wanted to hear his entire life. "I love you too, Pa." Jacob prayed with his father and Pa gave his life to Jesus just before he took his last breath. Jacob promised his father that he would bury Lucy between her father and mother.

Jacob's father's funeral was well attended. Even though he hadn't been kind and gentle with his family, he was still well-respected in the community. Jacob said a few words at the funeral about what a hard worker his father had been, and that he had always provided for his family. "Now Pa can be reunited with Ma and Lucy," he said at the end.

Jacob shed many tears for the loss of his father. Not for his death, because he knew he was now in Heaven, but mourning the loss of the time they could have had.

Several weeks after Pa's funeral, Jacob visited his parents' graves. It was a beautiful summer day and Jacob could hear robins singing as he walked to the cemetery. He had picked colourful wildflowers to put on his parents' graves. He even found sweet-smelling wild roses for Lucy's grave. They had been her favourite flowers. Jacob placed the flowers at the head of each grave. He said a prayer as he knelt down.

"Now you can be with Ma and Pa, dear Lucy," he whispered out loud, as he shed a tear and wiped it away quickly. Jacob had felt such relief since that day with his father. He hadn't had any more nightmares, and his heart felt at peace. Jacob stood up and wiped the dirt from his britches. He walked away feeling peaceful. He opened the gate of the churchyard and latched it behind him. As Jacob walked, he thought of the things that needed to get done that day. The wagon from Kingston was coming tomorrow to pick up the tables he had completed.

"Good day, Jacob," Mrs. Smyth said as they passed each other on Main Street.

"Good day," Jacob nodded.

"Hello there, Jacob," Reverend Young said as they met.

"Good day," Jacob nodded. *The streets are busy today*, he thought to himself. *It is a glorious day.* Jacob walked past The General Store and toward his house. Once he was inside, he saw a note on the table. *That wasn't there when I left*, Jacob told himself. He picked up the piece of paper and read it in bewilderment. There, in familiar handwriting, was a familiar poem. *It can't be. It couldn't be?* Jacob asked himself. *I have to find out.* Jacob reached for the latch on his door, opened it, and walked behind the hotel to his horse. He grabbed his saddle and placed it on her back.

"Hello, Jacob." That familiar British accent which had tickled his heart was music to Jacob's ears. Jacob turned around and was face to face with the beautiful English brunette who had first melted his heart.

"Abigail," Jacob whispered.

"Mama told me about your father, Jacob." Abigail gave her condolences; "I am so very sorry." She stepped closer to Jacob. He backed away, still stunned by her appearance.

"Well, that explains this." Jacob held out his hand with the folded paper. "What are you doing here?" He still couldn't believe his eyes.

"Mama kept me posted about how you have been doing ever since I left." Abigail avoided answering his question.

"I can't believe you are here, standing right before me. Where is your husband?" Jacob asked.

"Jacob. I just couldn't marry Patrick," Abigail blurted out as she put her arms around Jacob's neck. Her gentle touch and the smell of her hair made Jacob's heart flip flop, just as it had two years before. Jacob took her hands away from his neck and backed away. He couldn't touch a married woman like this.

"What do you mean?" Jacob asked, confused. "You were married last October."

"No, I wasn't," Abigail confessed.

"But your mother never said anything," Jacob persisted.

"I asked her not to," Abigail continued. "I never really loved Patrick. I mean, I thought I did."

"I don't understand," Jacob said, perplexed, as his heart pounded inside his chest with hope. "Why did you want to marry him?"

"Because I thought that we were in love," she cried in desperation. "Besides, it was what we were supposed to do, it was what we planned to do." Abigail was desperate to explain it to him; she could feel the distance between them. "Our parents expected it." Abigail and Patrick's parents had been close friends for a long time. They always envisioned that one day their children would marry. Abigail thought she loved Patrick, and she does, but as a brother not a husband.

"I have changed, Abigail." Jacob put his head down as he spoke. "A lot has happened since you left," he continued sadly.

"I know, Jacob," Abigail said softly. "I know." She knew of the incidents of the past year. Jacob looked at her with compassion.

"I love you," Abigail said tenderly. "I always have. I shouldn't have left you."

"If that is how you felt," Jacob seemed angry with her, "why did you ever leave?" He turned away from her and reached for his saddle.

"Jacob, please," Abigail pleaded. "I wanted to come back, but then Mama told me about your engagement."

"You had plenty of time before that," Jacob snapped as he tossed the saddle to the ground. He turned around and looked right at her. "I longed for you, Abigail. My heart broke for you. I needed you."

"You have every right to be angry," Abigail said quietly. "I didn't want to disappoint my parents. Please understand."

The desperation in her voice tugged at Jacob's heartstrings. "Can you forgive me?" she asked whole-heartedly. Jacob felt for Abigail but he wanted her to know that she had hurt him deeply. Jacob turned around and briskly walked toward the house, opened the door, and went inside. Abigail followed him and the door slammed shut behind her.

"Jacob, I really do love you." Abigail reached for him. Jacob didn't move. "But if there's nothing I can say to make you see, I can't do anything more." Abigail turned around and reached for the latch of the door and started to pull it open.

Jacob could feel the love stirring inside him. The love he had felt before, the love that had never really left him. That first love feeling. He walked up behind her and lifted his right hand and slowly pushed the door shut again. "Abigail," Jacob whispered. She turned around, leaning against the door, and he pulled her close, wrapping his muscular arms around her petite waist. He leaned down and pressed his lips gently to hers. It was a soft, gentle kiss, and it made him feel extraordinary inside. Their lips parted and Jacob slowly lifted his head. He gazed into Abigail's brown eyes. "I never stopped loving you." They embraced, and for a moment time stood still. It was as if time had never gone by.

THE END

Have you enjoyed Jacob of Abbington Pickets,
A Journey of Forgiveness?
Would you like to study God's word and
learn about forgiveness?
You may want to check out the
Bible Study Companion for Jacob of Abbington Pickets,
A Journey of Forgiveness. Study with a group or study solo.
Dig deeper into God's Word.
Go at your own pace, one chapter at a time.

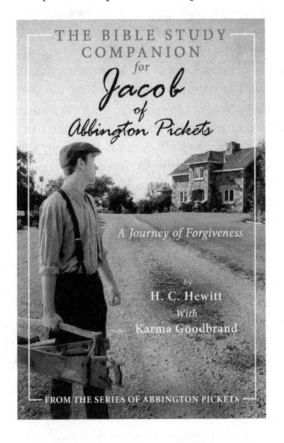

Available at www.hchewittauthor.com
or wherever books are sold.

Dear Readers,

I want to thank you for reading my first novel. This novel means more to me than you will ever know and I hope it will find a place in your heart. There is no doubt that I love history, and everything about it. Antiques are everywhere in my home. Not only antiques that are old, but antiques that are near and dear to me because they had once belonged to someone special in my family. However, when I receive a new antique, either by a relative, or a stranger, or whether I have purchased it myself, I always go through a process by researching it until I can't see straight. I want to know everything about it, where it came from, how old it is, what it's used for, and can I still use it? You get the idea! I want to know every detail, and until this happens, I am not yet satisfied. I have put some of these items in my book.

I like to feel and know what it was like to live a hundred years ago. Although my novel series is fiction, I want to tell you something. Some of my characters are real people. Special people. People I don't ever want to forget. I want to keep their memory alive by writing them into my stories and not letting their memory fade away. So, I have set them inside my story to let them live on in fiction. Alice and Bert Hibbert are my great grandparents, and they had a beautiful love story, I couldn't write a whole book on their life because it was just a little… as they say …too perfect. They were madly in love with each other and that was all there was to their happily ever after. But they were beautiful, kind, God loving people that influenced many, just as they are written in my book. I want them to live on forever in fiction.

God is my foundation. Without Him I am nothing. Bringing people to come to know Jesus, is my goal with my novels. If you need prayer, or want to talk about my novel, please feel free to contact me at any time.

Love and prayers, Corinne.

discussion questions

1. At a young age like Jacob's, how would you feel keeping a tragic secret about your father?

2. Would you be able to keep a secret like that?

3. Do you think his father knew Jacob knew his dark secret?

4. Jacob's father broke the table Jacob had made for his mama. How would you feel if your talent was dismissed, then destroyed? Was this the end of Jacob's efforts to be a good son?

5. How hard do you think it was for Jacob to leave his family to go and work at Goldenrod?

6. Do you think he should have left? Why?

7. When Abigail left, do you think she still intended to marry Patrick?

8. How would you feel if you were lost in a blizzard in the middle of nowhere, with no winter coats or many blankets?

9. Do you think Anna intentionally pursued Jacob at first? Or do you think she was just being a good neighbour?

10. Was that really normal for those times? Or did she risk her reputation?

11. What do you think the town thought of these two and how they were "carrying on"? Or do you think the town believed it was innocent?

12. If Jacob would have tried to mend fences with his father, how do you think he should have done it? Or should he have? Do you have people with whom you need to mend relationships?

13. Just think of a prairie fire, back in those days where they didn't have fire trucks and firemen to fight the fire. How would you feel in that situation?

14. After Anna died in the fire, Jacob's faith was lost, he was in a slump and no one seemed to get him out. How would you have felt in his situation?

15. It took Jacob's new friend Bert to show him that God doesn't fail, that all you need to do trust in Him. Once Jacob realized God has always been there, Jacob gave his life to Christ and was reborn. He got his life back. How would you feel? Have you given your life to Christ? Would you like to?

16. Would you have liked to have lived during Jacob's day? Or are you glad you live in today's world? Why?

17. How did you feel when Abigail came back?

18. How strong is your faith today? Can you think of situations in your life that may have paralleled Jacob's trying times?

19. Jacob forgave his father; how can we forgive and move on when we have been hurt so badly?

20. What is the best way to find peace and comfort in a tragic situation?

about the author

H. C. Hewitt grew up on a farm in Southeastern Saskatchewan where she developed a deep appreciation for the rural prairie landscape and the people who live there. She has been passionate about reading and writing from an early age and always knew that she would someday write a historical romance. Her grandmother's extensive knowledge of Saskatchewan history and her grandfather's collection  of antiques sparked an enduring love of history, especially of the era in which her story unfolds. Her story's setting in the series of *Abbington Pickets* was inspired by a historic park near where she grew up, founded in 1882 by an Englishman who set out to create a Victorian village in Canada.

H. C. Hewitt's other passion is quilting. She owns and operates a quilt shop where she designs and makes quilt patterns. Her four children have grown up and moved away, giving her more time for writing and quilting. She also has six grandchildren and loves to spend time with them. H. C. Hewitt lives in rural East-Central Alberta with her husband, dog, two cats, and nine miniature donkeys.

Corinne designs quilt and embroidery patterns to coincide with her novel series. Check out these and many other patterns including Canadian patriotic designs, at: www.hchewittauthor.com or connect with her at: hchewittauthor@gmail.com.

H. Corinne Hewitt
Pattern designer/Author

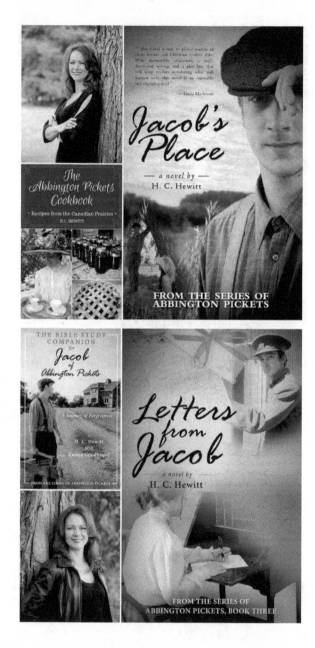

More books in the Abbington Pickets Series by H. C. Hewitt. You can find these on her website: www.hchewittauthor.com or wherever books are sold.

Connect with other Abbington Pickets fans or share by
using:
#abbingtonpicketsseries
#jacobofabbingtonpickets
#jacobsplace
#lettersfromjacob
#jacoblovesabigail
#joapbiblecompanion

You can also connect with Corinne on Facebook,
Instagram, and Twitter
@hchewittauthor

The Abbington Pickets Series